A Reason, A Season, A Lifetime

Traci Smith

This book is dedicated to my daughter

Courtney and my granddaughter Addison,

"You are my lifetimes."

Chapter One

"Friendship is a serious affection; the most sublime of all affections, because it is founded on principle, and cemented by time."- Mary Wollstencraft

Just one more time. Five more precious minutes on top of the ten she'd already taken would be guaranteed by hitting the snooze button just one more time. And she'd still make it on time. As she hit it, Elizabeth mentally reminded herself that she needed this part time job, the one requiring a 5 AM wake up on Sunday mornings. Her newly acquired mortgage and related homeowner expenses required more than the local school district offered to a third year teacher. The salary wasn't bad she supposed, based on what she'd heard from her other college graduate teacher friends but along with a brand new car payment, things were tight. Being 24 and single, these were the things that mattered.

Living at home with her parents two years following her college graduation had been hell but it had also allowed her to save enough of her teacher's salary to put a down payment on a two-bedroom townhouse. She really didn't need two bedrooms but she had been smart enough to realize that it would most likely be an advantage when she tried to sell it. Not that she was planning on doing that anytime soon, but she always looked at the big picture when there was one. And there always was one. This was a reality she had come to that also made her believe she was 'maturing.' Had she voiced this epiphany to her mother, however, her mother would not have agreed. Even though at age 24 Elizabeth had assumed a mortgage, qualified for a new car loan, and held a professional career position, her mother used every opportunity she could to tell Elizabeth that she had not yet reached maturity. After all, at age 24 her mother had been married six years and was expecting Elizabeth, her third child and only daughter. That, according to her mother, was an accurate measure of maturity. Her older brothers, both police officers in town, had already married and started their own families. Elizabeth cringed each time she tried to imagine herself in that scenario, and each time she became more and more thankful for the path her life was leading her on which was much different than that of her brothers.

There it was again, the annoying beep-beep-beep of the snooze alarm. She hated that sound. The five minutes had seemed like one but Elizabeth knew she couldn't hide under the covers any longer. To do so would mean there was no time for a shower and after a night out at Shorty's, one of the local popular bars, her hair would reek of smoke and the stale bar odors that accompany that environment. She didn't know how offensive it was to others but she hated the smell herself so a shower was a must. Funny, she could spend hours at Shorty's and it didn't bother her a bit but living with the staunch smell afterwards was a no-no for her. If her friends tried to point out the irony to her she'd brush them off. Elizabeth wasn't a mean person but she was very opinionated, strong-willed, and blunt. It took a lot for her to back down or accept someone else's opinion over her own. Unless it was a matter worth winning, her friends let it go each time and silently agreed to disagree.

Elizabeth groaned as she tossed the sheet off her body and stretched out her arms and legs. A yawn escaped her mouth, the one leftover from last night. Two or three hours of sleep were enough but she could always use more. She tried to remember if she had washed her waitress outfit from last Sunday. She hoped so. Otherwise she'd have to wear the traditional black pants and white blouse that trainees were required to wear until they'd earned the official uniform. The official uniform was nothing spectacular, a red, black and white dress made of polyester. In reality, it was quite hideous looking. But everyone knew it meant you weren't in training anymore when you wore one, and those in training when told they were graduating to the uniform knew it meant they weren't at risk of being let go anytime soon. Had the restaurant not been located right beside the Army Post where high ranking officials met daily, they wouldn't have catered to such a lucrative group and tips would not be nearly what they were. But the money was very good and because of that, the uniform meant everything. Elizabeth sat up and wiggled her way out of the full-wave waterbed she'd purchased when she bought the townhouse. Everyone had tried to convince her to get a semi-wave or wave-less but Elizabeth had wanted the full-wave before she walked into the store, so that's what she got without even trying out the others. She said it made her feel like she was riding a raft on the ocean and the beach was her favorite place to be, so the full wave made sense to her. Once upright, she shuffled over to her private bathroom and switched on the light. The other bathroom was the guest bathroom located out in the hall. First things first, relieve the bladder of the beer she'd consumed the night before. No doubt about it, Elizabeth had a cast iron stomach for partying when she wanted to.

Last night had been a lighter night though, just beer, but lots of it based on how long she had to sit there. Next she moved to the laundry basket located in her closet. Hurriedly, she rifled through the stack of dirty clothing praying she wouldn't come across the dress. As she dug she made a mental note to do laundry that afternoon. Most Sunday afternoons, no matter how well-planned or intentioned she was, were usually spent with some of the other Carriage House staff coming over to her place for a get-together. The restaurant closed at two on Sunday afternoons, a gift to those who worked that day. Sundays were their busiest day of the week due to the regular crowd from the military instillation plus the church crowd. For some reason the church crowd loved the Carriage House, probably because it was a non-smoking restaurant. It was a small restaurant and turnover was quick. From about 9:30 on there was almost always a waiting line.

They closed at two and clean up was usually done by three at the latest. Most employees were single, some younger, some older, and they were always looking for something to do. Their small Pennsylvania town, located about an hour from the closest large city, was a very family oriented small town and offered nothing for singles to do on the weekends, leaving them to find or create their own fun. Most people Elizabeth knew who hadn't settled down by now had migrated four hours east to the coast, choosing to live and work at the beach. She may have done so herself if she didn't love her teaching job so much. Mostly out of boredom, Elizabeth had taken it upon herself to set up the Sunday afternoon gatherings once she bought her townhouse. The only rule was that everyone had to bring something to eat, Elizabeth provided the beverages. The overflowing laundry basket was an issue though, and she'd have to do it while her friends were there later today.

Success! She finally reached the bottom of the basket without locating the uniform. This meant it was in her laundry room where she hung it to dry after washing it. Hanging it instead of drying it (thus forgetting it and letting it sit in the dryer for days on end) meant no wrinkles and therefore, no ironing. She decided to shower first and then go get the dress from the laundry room. One of the benefits of living alone was that she could walk around naked whenever she wanted. There were other benefits too, of course, like not having to sneak a guy in at night, not having to do the dishes right after eating if she didn't want to, but most of all, not having to hear her parents say, "You're 24 and you still live with us!" She loved the shocked look on her mother's face when she informed her she was not only moving out, but that she was buying a townhouse of her own with money she had saved herself. She and her mother loved each other but had never had a close relationship. People kept telling her that would happen later in life, when she realized all that her mother had done for her. Elizabeth was pretty sure she already realized all her mother had done for her; brought her into the world, raised her successfully throughout her schooling years, and paid for her four-year education to become a teacher. As far as Elizabeth was concerned that was it in a nutshell, she didn't know what realization she was supposed to have in the years to come but she was pretty sure Maureen Morrison had concluded her duties.

     Elizabeth took her shower quickly and dried off. Then she pranced naked down the hall and into the laundry room to retrieve her dress. It wasn't really a laundry room, it was a small closet with what she called a 'double decker' washer and dryer stuffed into it; washer on the bottom, dryer on the top. There was just enough room for a small garbage can in which to deposit the lint from the dryer's lint trapper and for her upright drying rack. She thought that constituted a laundry room and so she called it such. Back in her room, she quickly dressed and pulled her hair back into a ponytail, required by the new owners of the Carriage House. Made sense, she supposed, but she thought she looked so much better with her hair down. Try getting a guy to ask you out when you look like a 50's sock-hop girl with the ponytail and the ugly uniform as well as the white anklets and white waitress shoes they also required. Actually they were designed for nurses but waitresses wore them too. And they weren't cheap! Elizabeth was grateful for their comfort and support after a busy Sunday though, they did seem to help keep her feet from hurting so much with all the walking she did at the restaurant. Being one of the most seasoned waitresses on staff, she was the one they relied on to take extra tables and sometimes do double duty as cashier when the assigned one didn't show up for work. Of course they didn't pay her double but she didn't mind. It made her feel good that she was able to do it when many of the others weren't. It wasn't that they wouldn't want to, they just couldn't; they weren't as experienced as Elizabeth. She had waitressed her entire college career, summers too. Her parents paid for her education but she was required to provide her own spending money. So she worked. She worked hard. She liked and needed her spending money.

A quick brush with the makeup just to give her a little color and she was done. Elizabeth didn't wear much makeup; she didn't need it. She wasn't stark raving beautiful but she had great skin. Her friends had told her makeup would enhance her looks but she said that if God had wanted her to have makeup on, he would have put it on her before she was born. She knew that couldn't really happen and she wasn't overly religious or anything but it closed the subject with her friends pretty quickly. A glance at the clock and she was ready to go with about 11 minutes to spare. Damn it, she could've hit the snooze button one more time.

7

She seriously debated lying down and resetting the alarm for another ten minutes but in the end she decided to go in a little early. Mark, the early morning cook, wouldn't know how to act. She was usually pulling into the parking lot along with the first customer. She and Mark had a standing rule that for any customers he had to wait on before her arrival, he would get the tip and Elizabeth would have to double it. That had happened a few times but not too often that Mark minded. He was a good guy, recently married and usually in a pretty good mood. If he wasn't though, look out.

She remembered one time when a waitress in training had placed her first order. Being a small, traditional restaurant, the Carriage House was not automated or computerized. Everything was done the old fashioned way with waitress order pads including a duplicate you took to the kitchen when the order was placed. Also because of its small size, the Carriage House didn't have a system for calling waitresses to the kitchen. You were simply supposed to check back from time to time to see if you had an order up. It was a Sunday morning and the craziness of the usual Sunday morning had begun about 30 minutes prior to the new girl's order. She placed her order onto the spindle. When Mark pulled it off, he noticed that it said 'eggs.' That's it, just eggs. Two of the seasoned waitresses were in the back and heard Mark chuckle. They asked what was so funny and he told them what the waitress had done. He was busy but he was willing to take the time to explain to the new girl why this wasn't the proper way to order eggs. When she arrived in the kitchen, he called her to the side (waitresses were never allowed behind the line-Mark's rule) and told her he needed to know how the customer wanted the eggs prepared. She looked at him and said, "They just said eggs. I suppose you can make them any way you want."

Mark looked at her for a moment, trying to figure out if she was being funny or if she was really that stupid. Meanwhile the spindle continued to fill. He glanced first at it and then over at the other waitresses to try and garner their opinion but they were speechless and their faces said so. He looked back at her and tried again, "Hon, they either want them over light, over hard, scrambled, poached, something like that. I need you to go out there and ask them how they want their eggs done please." She turned around with a silent 'harrumph' as if she'd been defeated and marched out of the kitchen, only to return within five seconds.

"I'm too embarrassed to ask them. Just make them any way you want and if it's not what they want, I'll bring them back and you can make them again. And don't ever call me hon again." The other waitresses backed up knowing this wasn't going to fare well for anyone in the tiny kitchen, least of all the new waitress. Surprisingly, Mark stared at her for only a second or two and then reached for the tickets on the spindle and returned to his cooking responsibilities. Before long she walked back and asked if her order was ready. Mark didn't look up and said nothing but pointed his spatula to a plate in the window with two whole eggs, shell and all, sitting on it. The waitress careened her head into the food window and said, "What is this?"

Before anyone could inhale or exhale, Mark slammed his spatula down on the eggs which caused them to break open. When he did, raw egg splattered all over the girl's face, hair, and blouse as well as the inside walls of the food window .Mark yelled, "You ordered eggs, you got eggs. And since I can't call you hon, I'll just call you bitch!" Needless to say the new girl quit on the spot. Not a word was said to Mark and no one had the nerve to tell the owners. Honestly, they had all thought it was quite hilarious and said so as they helped Mark clean up the window area.

As she pulled into the parking lot, she saw Mark's familiar truck and one other vehicle. Shit, one customer had beaten her in even with her being early. Mark must've been in a good mood because he'd obviously taken the customer in, something he wasn't expected to do but sometimes did. If he was in a good mood. She was going to owe him double the tip. Maybe the guy would stiff him. Then she wouldn't owe him anything. Ha! Take that, she joked to herself. Serves you right for being so kind to the early bird.

She pulled between two spots in the back; she didn't like her new shiny black Camaro parked out there where hungry breakfast goers were quick to fling their doors open causing door dings. She assumed the fear would wear off eventually but for now the car still smelled new and so it mattered. She entered through the back which was where the freezers were. It was always cold out there, even on a nice summery August day like this one. As she opened the door and entered the kitchen, she heard conversation. Mark would never let a customer in the kitchen. She hoped nothing was wrong. If she hadn't been so impulsive she would have stopped to listen to the conversation first to try and determine who he was talking to and if everything was ok. Her wild imagination would later wonder - what if it was a robber? If she had stopped to listen first she could have figured it out, snuck out the back door and gone for help. She would have been a hero! But she wasn't one to stop and think first so she strode into the kitchen and headed toward the lockers to hang her purse up on a hook.

"Morning, Mark," she said glancing over her shoulder and toward his line. Then she saw the other person involved in the conversation. It was a female. She was young, pretty, and had quite a rack on her. Elizabeth was blunt like that, she wouldn't beat around the bush by saying the girl was 'well endowed' or had been 'blessed up top' or anything stupid like that. Life was too short. Just be honest from the start. BLUF. That was her motto. Bottom Line Up Front. She'd learned it from a customer who was an Army Officer and it was what she lived by, she wished others did too. The girl was standing beside the line, not behind it-Mark's rule. She was smiling happily. Elizabeth wondered who she was, Mark was married and this wasn't his wife. And then it hit her that the girl was dressed in training gear. The black pants and white blouse. Really, a new girl on a Sunday? What were the owners thinking? The busiest day of the week and they bring in a new girl for Elizabeth to train? Great, just great. And she had the nerve to make Elizabeth look bad by showing up before her. And why didn't the owners tell her she'd be training a new girl? She didn't mind doing it but for no reason she could think of she would have liked to have known. It wouldn't have made any difference except she might have tried to get there a little earlier. Then again, maybe not.

Mark returned the greeting with a smile, "Morning, Elizabeth. This is Amy." Amy, she thought. What a cute name. Cute name, cute girl, and big boobs to boot. Mark continued. "Amy's been working the dinner shifts Tuesday through Saturday but she's going to be starting a teaching job soon so she's only going to work Sundays from now on, starting today." A teacher, thought Elizabeth. Of all things we could have in common it has to be our career. Why couldn't it be the big boobs?

"Hi Amy, nice to meet you. You can follow me today since you're still in training, I don't mind." Amy smiled again and started to speak but Mark cut her off.

"She's not in training Elizabeth, she just didn't have time to wash her uniform since last night's shift." She should be a little more organized Elizabeth thought to herself, forgetting all about her morning search through the laundry basket for her own uniform. She wasn't sure why but she wasn't liking this whole Amy deal this morning. This wasn't usually like her but the whole thing caught her off guard and she assumed that's why she was feeling pissy.

"OK Amy, you know what you're doing then, have at it." Amy turned on her heel and looked at

Elizabeth. She wasn't sure how to take her. She was feeling a little bit of animosity and didn't know why. Surely she hadn't done anything. She hadn't even said anything yet. She looked at Mark for support but he just shot her a smile and went back to his work. She decided to take the bull by the horns. She followed Elizabeth out into the dining room where she saw her setting tables up with silverware. She was mumbling something about the evening girls not doing their jobs. The silver should've been set the night before and how was she supposed to get her own morning things ready if she had to do their job too?

Amy intervened, smiling. "Elizabeth, I worked last night and we had several really late tables. The silverware wasn't run by the time we finished up so I told everyone to leave and I'd do it this morning. I'm sorry. I wanted to get it done before you got here but…"

Elizabeth cut her off and the smile faded from Amy's face. Elizabeth glared at her as if they were ten years old and Amy had just stolen her best friend. "Why are you here so early? I'm the Sunday opener. Are they bringing two of us in now, because we don't need two openers. If that's the case I'll gladly sleep in another hour and you can open. Just let me know, I don't need to be here if I'm not needed." She continued to set the silver despite Amy's offer to do so. Amy made a wise decision not to try and intervene with the silver, she just let Elizabeth continue.

"The owners didn't tell me what time to come in Elizabeth. I knew we opened at 6 and to be safe, I

13

just came in then. I don't think it'll be my usual shift but I just didn't know. So here I am. What would you like me to do?"

Elizabeth turned and looked at her. Amy looked genuine and sincere and Elizabeth felt a little embarrassed about her own behavior. She hated when she got like this. It was her impulsiveness again. Something would happen and she would react before anyone had a chance to tell her anything. She attributed it to something from her childhood, she wasn't sure what but she tended to blame her parents, probably her mother in particular. Her father was the silent partner, he was a 'Yes Maureen, no Maureen' kind of guy. Never a conflict, never a disagreement, just go along to keep the peace. Taking a deep breath Elizabeth said, "Oh God Amy I'm sorry. I don't know what's with me today, it's not like I'm PMSing or anything but I feel like a total bitch. I didn't feel that way til I walked in the kitchen, I mean, it's not because of you or Mark or anything but…"

This time it was Amy who interrupted Elizabeth. She smiled and said, "Don't worry about it. I have mornings like that too. This morning stuff is new to me having worked only evenings before. I really need you to tell me what to do, mornings are different than evenings, I can already tell just by the things you're doing." Elizabeth let out a huge sigh of relief. Amy wasn't trying to take over, in fact she needed Elizabeth's help. OK, this was going to be ok.

Her hands still full of silverware, she nudged her elbow toward the small refrigerator and told Amy what to get out of it, where to put it, and a few other things to prepare. Amy set straight to the tasks Elizabeth had given her. Elizabeth noticed that Amy hummed as she worked. That wouldn't last long once the rush hit, she'd be too busy to hum. Elizabeth's attention was averted to the clang of the tiny bell attached to the entry door. A customer. Good, once the day started it went quickly.

Elizabeth recognized him as a regular customer, he was usually one of the first to come in on Sundays. He was nice enough, easy to wait on and usually left a dollar. Keep their coffee refilled and they're happy, that's what Elizabeth told all the new girls she helped to train. She told them there's no reason they can't pull at least a dollar tip off of every person who came in alone, more off deuces and parties of three or more. Just pay attention to them, keep their coffee full, and smile. Easy.

Elizabeth and Amy both greeted their first customer at the same time. Since Amy was first in, her name went first on the rotation list so this would be her table. Elizabeth wrote their names in, Amy's first. Slight pang of irritability, Elizabeth usually had all the tables from six until seven when the next person was scheduled to come in. Suck it up, she told herself as she placed a stroke by Amy's name, indicating a table had been given. "How about we put you over here today, a nice table by the window? Amy is our new Sunday morning waitress and she'll be right with you. I'll tell her you like your coffee with lots of cream." The man smiled and settled into his seat, adjusting the silverware and placemat to his liking. There are only

15

so many ways to move that stuff but customers did it all the time, like it was a puzzle or a map or something.

As she approached Amy to tell her about the man's coffee, Amy spoke first. "Elizabeth, why don't you take him? You know him and he's obviously used to you, go ahead." Great, fine with her, she thought.

"OK, thanks," Elizabeth said with a smile as she grabbed a coffee mug, filled it, snatched a handful of creamers out of the ice and headed to the man's table. The little bell chimed again, Elizabeth turned her head out of instinct and she and Amy's eyes met. For some reason Elizabeth's entire attitude changed right that second. All of a sudden she was glad to have Amy there. She suddenly didn't mind sharing her first morning tables. Why though? She didn't have a clue, but suddenly she felt happy.

They continued to stare at each other for a brief second, then Elizabeth said, "Go ahead Amy, you're up," and smiled as she returned to her own customer. As Amy seated her customers, Elizabeth headed to the kitchen with her order. Mark hated when the waitresses spindled their orders if he was standing right there doing nothing so Elizabeth spindled it just to irritate him. It worked. He snatched it off the spindle so hard it ripped. They both just smirked at each other, they had worked together long enough to be able to joke like this.

"What do you think of Amy?" Mark asked. Elizabeth wondered why he was asking that question, it was a strange one coming from him. He usually couldn't care less about the waitresses, what they did,

16

if they liked each other. Mark had not attended any of Elizabeth's Sunday functions, he spent the time with his wife. They often wondered if Mark and/or his wife thought they were too good for the rest of them. They didn't know his wife too well but Mark could be standoffish at times.

Still wondering what his intent was behind the question, Elizabeth replied, "She's ok. Seems nice. I apologized to her for being so mean earlier. I'm sure we'll be just fine together." She paused a second and then said, "Why did you ask me that?" Mark looked at her with a very serious face .

"Elizabeth, I don't know why but having worked with her occasionally when I fill in at nights and having worked with you each Sunday, I have a feeling you two could be really good friends. You have a lot in common and your strengths and weaknesses complement each other. I'll be curious to see where this goes." Holy crap, Elizabeth thought. Mark philosophizing? Since when has he ever taken notice of people or even cared about them interacting? And what was this with strengths and weaknesses? Guess he has a lot of spare time behind that window. And what did he mean, 'see where this goes?' She was nearly dumbfounded and didn't know what to say. Mark must've sensed it as he smiled at her with a wink and turned to begin cooking her order.

Still slightly taken aback by Mark's comments, Elizabeth walked back out to the front part of the restaurant. Amy was finishing up her order with her table of four, a mom, a dad, and two kids. The kids were well behaved so far, Elizabeth hated when kids were out of control and parents did nothing. It was the teacher in her. She loved kids, as long as they weren't hers. Elizabeth noticed that Amy was smiling again, she did that a lot. Still humming too, seemed like she hummed anytime she wasn't talking. Assuming Amy was headed to the kitchen with her order, Elizabeth stepped aside.

She was momentarily confused when Amy veered off the path to the kitchen and stepped to the side where Elizabeth was standing. Holding a coffee pot in one hand and excess creamers in the other, Amy said, "Elizabeth, I've heard about your Sunday gatherings after work and if it's ok for me to come, I made a marble cheesecake yesterday that I'd like to bring. Is that ok?" Amy kind of dug her head down into the nape of her neck and scrunched up her face as she asked, like a child begging forgiveness instead of asking permission.

This time Elizabeth smiled first. "Of course, it's open to anyone. You can carpool, follow someone, or I can write directions down for you, just let me know." Amy replied that directions would suffice and then as she glanced out the restaurant window, she groaned. Elizabeth's eyes followed her view out the window and saw a couple getting out of their car. "What?" Elizabeth asked.

Amy sighed and said, "My parents. They're coming in for breakfast." Elizabeth's folks never came into the restaurant, too old fashioned, eating out was for rich people and they weren't rich, they said. Probably another sign of maturity according to her mother, Elizabeth thought with a laugh.

18

"I'm sure you'll want to wait on them even though it's my turn and that's perfectly ok," Elizabeth told her. Amy rolled her eyes, then a smile slowly crossed her face. She hurriedly pushed Elizabeth toward the door .

"No, tell them we go in rotation and it's your turn. Tell them I can't take them, it would put us out of rotation. You take them, don't worry, they tip well." Confused, Elizabeth allowed Amy to push her toward the door, then watched Amy run to the kitchen. Before she could process it all, the couple was in the door. They introduced themselves as Amy's parents, Lois and Pete. Elizabeth seated them, explained the rotation procedure, asked if that would be ok, seated them and then took their order while Amy fussed around in the back pretending to cut fresh fruit.

When Elizabeth went to the kitchen to spindle her order, she grinned at Amy and asked, "So what's the big deal? You don't want to spend time with your parents?" Amy rolled her eyes again but smiled at the same time.

"I'd like to spend time *away* from them." She hesitated briefly, then said with a grin, "I live with them." Elizabeth stopped dead in her tracks. She knew all too well what that was like, being an adult trying to live in a house where the people treat you the only way they ever have, like a child. Suddenly she felt for Amy, badly. She walked over and reached out to hug her. Amy reached out and hugged her back.

Elizabeth laughed as she said, "Girlfriend, I know exactly how you feel," and they both laughed while Mark watched the interaction with interest from behind the line.

The rest of the shift went smoothly, busy but trouble-free. Elizabeth checked out right on schedule and headed home to prepare for the Sunday ritual but not before making sure that Amy had directions *and* planned to come for sure. Amy promised she'd be there. Elizabeth left with a smile on her face and in her heart which was unusual for her, all she knew was that she was very happy. Almost as happy as when she got asked out on a date. But this wasn't a date, why the happy feeling?

On her drive home, she stopped by the grocery store and grabbed beer and wine coolers. She also grabbed some sodas in case Gina brought her kids again. Cute they were but Elizabeth was never sad when they didn't come along. Gina, a single parent, didn't have the best parenting skills and as a teacher, it bothered Elizabeth. Suddenly she wondered if it would bother Amy too since she was planning on teaching. Why did she wonder that? What did she care what would or would not bother Amy?

Moving toward the checkout, she pushed the thoughts of Amy from her mind. As she drove the rest of the way home, she thought about her day, something she did from time to time. Her Sunday school teachers, when she attended years before, had called it 'reflecting' and said it was a good habit to put your day into perspective and perhaps find your purpose or meaning for the day. Pretty deep but whatever, Elizabeth had thought. As she reflected back on meeting Amy, she thought of something similar that her mother had always said to her, "People come into your life for a reason, a season, or a lifetime. You won't always know which one it is, sometimes it takes awhile to know and sometimes you may never know. But mark my words, it's true," she'd say. As Elizabeth downshifted and pulled her Camaro into her assigned parking spot marked by her townhouse number on the curb, she wondered for which one of those Amy had entered her life, and how long it would take her to figure it out.

Chapter Two

"The language of friendship is not words but meanings." – Henry David Thoreau

The Sunday gathering went off as usual without a hitch. That's how it generally went; people came over, had a few drinks, ate a bit, socialized and left. Gina's kids were actually fairly well behaved except for the incident with the sliding glass patio door, which in the end was pretty funny. Living on the first floor had its benefits, one of which was being able to walk out into a grassy area. The Sunday crew would mingle from inside to out and the patio door usually remained open. Carter, one of the newer cooks and spending his first Sunday with the gang, instinctively pulled the sliding door shut when he came in just before Gina's daughter went to run out. BAM! She smacked right into the glass door and bounced back about two feet to the floor. Gina immediately gasped and ran to her, everyone else gasped and just sat there. It was one of those things that looked so funny you just wanted to howl with laughter but until you're sure everyone's ok, you really can't. So everyone just sat there until Gina said something motherly that let everyone know all was well and then the laughter erupted, including some from Gina. It was just enough excitement to end a weekend and prepare to start the work week all over again. Amy seemed to fit in nicely, sitting quietly and taking in the conversation, adding her two cents worth here and there. And from the little Elizabeth had heard, she was kind of funny.

In-service week for teachers would start in another week so Elizabeth had one week left to enjoy the summer sun. Her plans to go to the beach one last time, her favorite place of all, were spoiled by her mother who had planned a special shopping trip for the two of them. Elizabeth agreed to go only because her mother would insist on buying things for her. The major downside was staying at her aunt's house. It was too expensive to shop *and* stay in a hotel according to her mother. As she packed her suitcase for the overnight trip she thought about what would be happening at the beach that week, would Mr. Right be there and she'd miss him? Figures, it would be just her luck to miss out on the man of her dreams due to her mother's interference. The last two times she went to the beach she was sure she had met Mr. Right, both times, but Leo turned out to be married, what an asshole liar, and John turned out to be into one night stands. It just so happened he'd honored her with three of them in a row which led her to believe he wanted a relationship. Each time she came home she swore she'd never pick up a guy at the beach again, after all they were all on vacation and looking for the same thing-a good time, not a long time. Referring back to her mother's saying, these guys obviously came into

23

her life for a reason. What that reason was remained to be seen but Elizabeth thought it must have something to do with holding out hope that Mr. Right, AKA her lifetime, could be out there somewhere.

Returning her thoughts to her trip, she knew that spending the time with her mother could be somewhat enjoyable if she got in the usual cuts, 'not sure if I'll ever get married...not sure if I want kids...' The truth was Elizabeth wanted a husband; kids she could do without but a house, a dog, the whole nine yards, yes, eventually, and she knew it was what her mother wanted for her too and sooner rather than later. So just to irritate her mother and give her something new to worry about, she'd mention from time to time that her thoughts weren't clear on these issues. Her mom doted on her niece and nephews and often commented that she couldn't wait for Elizabeth to add to the brood. The truth was Elizabeth wasn't clear on the kid part of it. She just knew that kids would take up so much of her time and so much attention away from her, why do that to herself?

Her mother, seeing additional grandchildren dissipating from her future as they spoke, would frantically begin to point out the cons of being alone with no husband, no children, and often posed the question, 'who would take care of you?' Elizabeth often wanted to say, 'I am perfectly capable of taking care of myself, and just how would you know what that would be like anyway? You've had someone taking care of you your entire life, going from the high school graduation stage to the chapel, so just how would you know what it's like not to have someone

24

taking care of you?' Mostly out of respect for her mother, she never said it aloud. She loved her mother, didn't necessarily agree with her ways or her style, but she loved her nonetheless.

She realized she'd been standing over her suitcase with a pair of shorts in her hands for the last three minutes as she thought all of this through and quickly banished the thought of having kids from her mind with a shudder. She tossed the last of her things into the small suitcase and snapped it shut. She hated this luggage, it had been her parent's gift to her upon her graduation from high school. Light blue vinyl with white polka dots, how little-girlish. And while most of her friends got cars, jewelry, or better yet, cash for graduation, she got luggage. That was her parent's style, practicality. She'd need the luggage to get her things to college, her mother had said. In all reality she had never thought about how to get her things to college but she was sure she could've done it without the three piece vinyl *Tourister* luggage set.

Hoisting the suitcase in her hand, she turned to leave the bedroom just in time to hear the landline ring. Perfect she thought, it'll be mom, no one else ever calls the landline, and she'll tell me something's come up, we can't go and I can still make it to the beach. Dropping her suitcase on the floor, she flopped across her waterbed and reached for the phone. "Hello," she said sounding a little impatient and irritated. If it was her mother she wanted her to know she was bothering her. The voice on the other end came across with a response that immediately let her know it wasn't her mother.

"Hi Elizabeth, is this a bad time?" Her mother never would have cared enough to ask about the timing so despite the fact that it wasn't her mother's voice, she knew it couldn't have been her even if she had disguised it for some reason. She knew the voice on the line but couldn't place it. Think, Elizabeth, think, she hated not knowing something or having the feeling that she didn't have the upper hand. Before she could put two and two together the voice continued, "It's me, Amy, I hope you don't mind me calling, I got your number from the restaurant…"

Elizabeth lay still on the bed, unsure what to do or say, wondering why she would've listed her landline as her number with the restaurant. Unwilling to let Amy know she was clueless a second ago, she interrupted her and went with the obvious. "Oh hi Amy, I thought it was you, kinda busy but I have a quick sec, what's up?" She'd saved face and did so quite cool and calm like, if she did say so herself.

Amy went on to tell her that she wanted to thank her for the hospitality the evening before and wondered if they could get together sometime to talk about teaching. It was going to be Amy's first year and she'd really appreciate someone with some experience giving her some heads-up information on the reality of the job. Elizabeth felt herself grinning as she replied, feeling the all too familiar feeling of being the one in the know. Again, not a cocky feeling, just the 'I know what she needs to know' thing. "Sure, be happy to, teaching's a lot of fun. Hard work too, but fun. I'm headed out of town for a few nights with my mom but when I get back I can give you a call, how's that sound?"

Amy's tone changed with her next response. "Oh my God, can I come with you? I'd do anything to get away from my mother for a night, even if it meant being around someone else's." Elizabeth startled back from her end of the receiver and gave it a distorted look. Did she just invite herself to come along with us, she thought? Surely she's kidding. "I'm kidding of course," Amy continued, "I just can't stand living at home." To this Elizabeth could certainly relate. She remembered all too well the fights with her parents when she lived at home. Twenty one years old with a curfew? Having her breath sniffed when she walked in at 2 AM? Questions about who she was with, whose phone number was scribbled on the back of her hand, who was the person in the car that dropped her off and where's your own car, by the way? No thanks, no more of that for her.

"Listen, I'll get in touch with you when we get back, ok? Should only be a few days and we'll still have time before in-service week starts." There it was, Elizabeth in control, just like she liked it.

"Sure," Amy said, "don't have too much fun," she added before Elizabeth got the final word in.

"I never do when I'm with my mom." Before she could end the call though, Amy chimed back in.

"Do you think our moms might've been twins separated at birth? Sounds like we both get the same kind of crap from them."

Without a second's hesitation Elizabeth responded, "Oh my God, you have no idea. The best thing I ever did was get out of my parent's house. Still live in the same zip code, that makes them happy, but the little bit of distance is the best thing in the world. And hey, you have a job now, why don't you move out?" If only it were that simple, Amy thought. She wouldn't admit it to Elizabeth having just met her, but she already saw Elizabeth as some kind of idol to worship. Only three years in the real world (that's what it's called when you get out of college, or so they say) and she already owned her own place with no parents in sight. If ever Amy had a goal set for herself, this would be it.

"Maybe one day soon," Amy replied. "Maybe I can learn from you, you know, how to save, how to find a place without getting ripped off, you know, the details." Elizabeth beamed at the thought that once again, someone would be relying on her to lead them in the right direction. She smiled also at the thought of Amy, wondering what Amy would be doing for the next few days.

Before she knew it her mouth opened and she said, "So what are you up to the next few days?"

"Not much, I'll just hang out and watch TV. I might call a friend to go to a movie. Most of my friends have boyfriends which leaves me either out of the loop or a third wheel, neither of which is very fun." Unbelievable, another commonality! Elizabeth felt exactly the same way about her own friends, and sometimes felt used by them, especially Lindsay. When she was dating someone you didn't hear from

28

her but as soon as it went south, the phone would ring. And it would continue to ring for a few days until she found a new guy. She never seemed to be without a guy for very long and Elizabeth could never figure that out. Sure, she was cute, petite, fun, but so was Elizabeth, why did it happen so easily for Lindsay and not for her? Carrie on the other hand wasn't like that, even if she did date someone she would still call and hang out with Elizabeth which suited Elizabeth just fine. With Carrie she didn't mind being a third wheel because she had the knack to make the guy feel like he was in the way, not her. She didn't hesitate to share her thoughts on the current guy Carrie was with either; she was, if nothing else, protective of her friends. She remembered the guy Carrie fell head over heels with a few years ago, Dave, and how she saw him out with another girl one night after telling Carrie he had to help his grandmother move some things from her recently sold house to a one-bedroom apartment. Had all the details mapped out and everything. Unfortunately for him Elizabeth went to an out-of-the-way bar on a whim that night with a friend and ran right into him and his date. After her display she doubted that girl would ever want to talk to Dave again and Elizabeth wasted no time calling Carrie to inform her. Of course Carrie cried and Elizabeth felt bad but she knew that in the long run, Carrie would be thankful for her protective and brutally honest friend. And in time, she was. Carrie and Lindsay. Seasons, she supposed. It seemed they'd been friends most of their lives, Carrie since first grade and Lindsay since junior high so they were more than reasons, but Elizabeth just didn't see them as lifetimes. She knew that once they all got married Lindsay and Carrie would each start having kids right away, they'd said they would, and they'd all go their separate ways because Elizabeth and her husband, childless, would have nothing in common with them.

Returning back to the conversation, Elizabeth tuned in to what Amy was saying, something about a friend who just got engaged and is never available anymore. "I know how you feel, I'm in the same boat most of the time."

And again, before she knew who or what was moving the muscles in her mouth, Elizabeth said, "Maybe you and I can go out for a beer when I get back." Whoa! Where did that come from, she thought frantically, looking around the room as if there was a demon with her forcing the words out of her mouth. Elizabeth never initiated that kind of stuff, it was always friends calling her to do things, friends asking her to go out for a beer. Elizabeth never showed desperation by asking someone to do anything with her. What in the world was happening here?

"That would be great! Just give me a call when you get back, did my cell number show up on your caller ID?" It had.

Elizabeth, still reeling from her outburst of words a moment earlier, said, "Yes, it did, and ok, I will. Hey my dryer chimer is going off so I gotta go. See ya." With that she hung up. This allowed her to have the last word, which made her feel superior in the conversation despite the fact that her dryer wasn't even running at the time.

The trip with her mother went by quickly and so did the remaining time before school started. Elizabeth didn't call Amy as she had promised; in all honesty Elizabeth had forgotten about it. She had her own things to take care of and prepare for as the new school year was beginning. It was the final day of in-service training and Elizabeth was transitioning from one room to another for some more of the routine 'sit and git' information. They brought professional consultants to jam information down teacher's throats every year right before school started. Did they really think anyone listened, or better yet, cared about this stuff? Every teacher in the room was thinking about how much they had to do to get their room ready for kids. Throughout the presentations people could be seen doodling, writing grocery or to-do lists, dozing off. Elizabeth could've sworn she saw one person filing her nails but she was at the other end of the room and couldn't be sure. The only ones who seemed alert and interested were the presenters. After all, the teachers were the ones who had to face kids in a few days, not these people. No wonder they were smiling.

As Elizabeth entered room 17B, the room that hosted the last session she'd have to attend for the day, she looked around for a familiar face to sit with. If you had someone to whisper with or jot notes back and forth to, the time went faster. Funny, these are the exact things her own teachers yelled at her for in school and now as a teacher, she and her colleagues

31

were doing the same things. She glanced by the windows and saw no one she'd want to sit near. Her eyes traveled to the back of the room and then began to scan the middle section. Her gaze stopped when she spotted a good looking guy she had not seen before. The district she worked for was small so she knew he was new. Well, well, well, not such a bad way to end the day, sit yourself beside the new guy who just happens to be hot and possibly leave with a date for the weekend.

As she sauntered down the aisle to take a seat beside him, she nearly tripped over a huge purse that was blocking her path. Disgusted with the purse owner's disregard, she gasped loudly and grasped at the desk as if to show that this inconsiderate person had nearly caused her to fall. The purse owner looked up immediately and began to apologize but stopped short before saying, "Elizabeth, how are you?"

Oh great. It was Amy. Now the questions would start. Why hadn't Elizabeth called her, would she sit with her, was she busy this weekend, could she help her with some new teacher things. Why oh why did it have to be Amy? Elizabeth forced a smile to her face while trying to see if the hot guy a few rows back had seen her little act.

"I was doing great til I nearly broke my neck here Aim, how about yourself?"

Amy once again began the apology, this time finishing it, before saying, "I'm great, but all this information. Ugh. I don't know when I'll have time to do anything with any of it."

"You won't," Elizabeth told her with a knowing smirk, "just put it all in a file and toss it when you feel comfortable that you've survived without it."

Amy motioned to the seat beside her, "Here you go Elizabeth, have a seat." She shot one more eye toward the hot guy, who she didn't think was paying any attention to her so she shrugged and took the seat.

The in-service session ended and the girls headed to the door. "Excuse me," came a voice from behind them. They both turned to see hot guy walking toward them. Oh my God, maybe he was paying more attention than I knew, Elizabeth thought. He approached her first. God, he was gorgeous. He had the darkest eyes she'd ever seen and they glistened as the sun hit them through the windows. His hair was jet black and wavy, styled perfectly but not too GQ-ish.

The man introduced himself as Lance Smith as the girls shared their own names. Small talk ensued and it turned out all three of them would be teaching in the same building. Great, thought Elizabeth. Now if she could just get rid of Amy, she could get to know him a little more personally. No sooner had she finished the thought and Amy announced that she had to get going. She had agreed to take on an extra shift at the Carriage House and although she now regretted it, she was committed.

"Okay," Elizabeth almost yelled happily, "see you there Sunday." Lance and Elizabeth began walking and talking and before they left the building, he had indeed asked her out to dinner. He alluded to the fact that he'd like to get some insight into the district, he had taught before but was new to the district and just had a few questions. Use whatever excuse you want, Elizabeth thought, you know you like me, which was just fine because Elizabeth liked him, too.

Dinner with Lance went better than she could have imagined and before she knew it they had been dating for two months. She had no mixed feelings either, typically she would whenever she dated someone for longer than a week or two but with Lance, she was convinced he was the one for her. They had everything in common including the fact that both had two brothers and no sisters, they were both good looking, had excellent careers, and even her mother seemed to approve although she hadn't officially met him yet, she was basing her opinion on what she'd heard from Elizabeth.

Elizabeth was also striking up more of a friendship with Amy. They had met for lunch a few Saturdays and had gotten to know each other a little better through working together at the restaurant on Sundays. Lance had started stopping in to Elizabeth's 'after work' get-together events and everyone seemed to like him. Even if they didn't, they wouldn't tell Elizabeth but they genuinely did like him. He did nice things for Elizabeth, unexpected things, things that made everyone say, "Aww, isn't he sweet?" Flowers for no reason, washing her car without her knowing, arranging for a weekend getaway to her favorite place, the beach, and having Amy arrange for someone to cover her shift at the restaurant. Life was good for Elizabeth and Lance and everyone suspected it was headed somewhere.

After about five months of dating, Elizabeth had a scare. She had missed her period and initially didn't even realize it but when she had, she panicked. It was a Sunday morning, she had gone to work as usual and Amy was the first one at the restaurant to say anything to her. "What is wrong with you, Elizabeth? Mark said you've messed up three orders, a customer complained that you spilled coffee on him, and you've barely said two words to anyone all morning. What's going on?"

She looked into Amy's eyes with no idea what words would come out of her mouth and was surprised to feel tears welling up in her eyes. Elizabeth was not an emotional person and didn't cry easily or often. Amy took her by the arm and pulled her back into the kitchen, past the cook line, and into the dry stock pantry. She pulled the door shut behind her and took Elizabeth by the arm.

"What is it? Is it Lance? Did you two break up? Have a fight? Is he cheating on you?" All Elizabeth could do was shake her head. "Well what then, what is wrong?"

Elizabeth had never had a close friend as a confidant. She had never needed one. Sure, she'd had girlfriends but none of them ever measured up to the level of telling them she might be pregnant. Carrie and Lindsay were probably her closest friends in life but never in a million years would she confide something like this in them. So having known Amy for less than a year, she was shocked when she heard the words come out of her mouth, "I think I'm pregnant," and then the tears flooded down her cheeks.

Amy, partially in shock herself, stared at her friend for a few seconds and then pulled her close and hugged her tightly. She wrapped her arms around her and rubbed her back in a soothing way. "Oh Elizabeth, it's going to be ok, calm down, calm down."

When Elizabeth had stopped crying enough to talk, she said, "I don't know how this happened. We use protection, double protection actually. I have a diaphragm and he uses condoms. How could this happen?"

Amy let her go on for a few more seconds and then interjected, "OK, hold on, let's not jump the gun. Have you taken a test?" No, was the stifled response. Just then the door opened and Mark appeared in the doorway. His stride had him heading to a shelf but he stopped mid-step. He took one look at the girls, turned his back to them and asked them to hand him a box of pancake mix. They did and he stepped back out. He didn't want any part of anything that had to do with girls crying and hugging. He just wasn't comfortable with it.

When the door shut again Amy took control. "OK Elizabeth, we're cancelling today's after work party and going to get a pregnancy test. Does Lance know?" Elizabeth shook her head, he did not. She told Amy that Lance would probably be thrilled and insist they get married and start their family now. He thought kids were the greatest, it was the one thing they didn't have in common yet she hadn't brought the difference to his attention yet but she would, in her own way. Sure, she would marry Lance, she was sure he was the one and was fairly confident he felt the same way about her, but not knowing if she even wanted kids she certainly didn't want to start out a marriage with one.

Amy sighed heavily and grabbed a tissue from her pocket. "Here," she said as she handed Elizabeth the tissue. "Get yourself cleaned up and come on back out. Start spreading the word that the party is cancelled. Say you don't feel good and maybe you can even get sent home a little early." Great, Elizabeth thought, faking morning sickness and I don't even know if I'm pregnant yet. She rationalized that it would be just her luck to pretend something like that and for lying, God would punish her for making it true. But she knew it didn't work that way. She was either pregnant or she wasn't. She prayed she wasn't.

After their shifts Amy had gone and purchased the test, Elizabeth said she was too embarrassed. The girls sat together in the bathroom of Elizabeth's townhouse, she on the toilet with her head down and Amy on the side of the bathtub holding the processing pregnancy stick. She had done what Amy read to her from the directions, started to pee and then inserted the stick and let the urine run over the end of it for five full seconds. How humiliating! She had never been in this kind of situation before. All she could think about was how a baby would ruin everything. She was sure she'd love it well enough like parents are supposed to but it surely wasn't part of her plans. The seconds seemed to tick by like hours until finally Amy said, "It's time."

Those words echoed in Elizabeth's head like vibrations from a bell tower. She asked her friend to read it for her, she just couldn't do it, and then began to silently cry as if she knew the answer already. Amy turned the stick over while simultaneously rubbing Elizabeth's back with her other hand. The room was so quiet it was deafening until Amy said one word.

"Elizabeth." Elizabeth didn't move, didn't say a word, she didn't even take a breath during that instant. "Elizabeth," she said again, "look at me." After a mental debate she sat up slowly, hair lingering in her face, a few wisps sticking to her moistened cheeks and lips, until she could see her friend's face. Amy was sitting on the tub, pregnancy stick in hand raised up in front of her, with the biggest smile on her face that Elizabeth had ever seen her display. While Elizabeth was trying to calculate everything she was seeing, Amy screamed, "You aren't pregnant! It's negative! You're not pregnant! Elizabeth, it's all ok, you aren't pregnant!"

Elizabeth reached out and snatched the stick from Amy's hand as she slowly started to stand. She pulled the stick in front of her to read the words for herself. NOT PREGNANT. There they were. The two best words in the world. NOT PREGNANT. The tears continued to stream down her face but this time for a different reason, she was not pregnant and her life was not going to be ruined. Amy grabbed her and hugged her, offering congratulations, and Elizabeth hugged her back, hard. Elizabeth had shown Amy

38

another side of her. She didn't pretend that this wasn't her, that this wasn't what she was like emotionally, that she didn't appreciate all that her friend had just gone through with her, but no words would come out of her mouth. Amy sensed it all and knew. She just knew. And as both girls hugged and cried tears of joy, Elizabeth's memory flooded back to the first day she met Amy many months ago. There had been something about her, about their connection, she wasn't sure what it was but there had been something. Most of the friends in her life so far had been there for reasons. She did a quick mental scan of her bank of friends and as much as she liked them, she couldn't have imagined going through this with any of them. It was at this moment that Elizabeth knew she had yet another friend who was more than a reason, Amy must be a season.

Chapter Three

"Friends show their love in times of trouble, not in happiness." -Euripides

The days, weeks, and months flew by and the school year was about to end. All three had had a fabulous year with their students and Amy was ecstatic that her first year was officially over, and successful. Amy and Elizabeth were still working together at the restaurant each Sunday and Elizabeth and Lance had fallen in love. The 'three little words' had been uttered after a passionate night of love-making on yet another weekend getaway to the beach, all planned by Lance. He doted on Elizabeth and she loved it. He made her feel like the center of the world and she never wanted that to change. She knew she'd found her lifetime.

Once or twice he had mentioned 'their kids'- speaking of futuristic children, of course – about how he hoped their little girl would look like Elizabeth and that their son would be athletic. He looked forward to hectic schedules, car pools, and all the firsts. Elizabeth hadn't a clue what he was referring to until he started giving examples, first steps, first tooth, first word, first day of school, first date. Blah, she thought, who cares about that stuff? Elizabeth had smiled each time their futuristic kids came up as if to acknowledge his thoughts, then each time, she successfully brought the conversation back to the present. She enjoyed her niece and nephews tremendously but couldn't imagine them being her own, going home with her, her being responsible for them. She knew this was every woman's dream but it wasn't hers and Lance would need to know that. In her mind, he would come around to agreeing with her when she mentioned it, which she'd do when the time was right.

The summer ended as quickly as it arrived and before long it was time for school to start again. Elizabeth, Amy and Lance all returned to the same building together and were often termed the Three Muskateachers by colleagues. They sat through the required in-service sessions again and thought back to the previous year when they'd all been virtual strangers to each other. So much had happened in a year. School was starting earlier this year so in-service was earlier as well, about a week before Lance and Elizabeth's one year dating anniversary. It was no surprise to anyone when Lance proposed to Elizabeth on the actual one year milestone date. What was a surprise was the way he did it.

First he sought the approval of her parents, which was given without any hesitation. Her parents adored Lance, having met him about six months into the relationship, right after the pregnancy scare. Her mother thought Lance reminded her a lot of her father when he was younger, handsome, ambitious, goal oriented, courteous and polite, every parent's dream for their daughter. When Lance sought their permission to marry, it was granted, and Elizabeth's mother immediately set the wheels turning in her own mind, first comes love, then comes marriage… Her father was a little emotional, Elizabeth was his only daughter after all, but he had grown fond of Lance and knew he would be a good husband for her. She was never really a daddy's girl but he did love her very much. However, he liked Lance a lot and knew Lance would provide a stable and happy life for Elizabeth so his permission to ask for his only daughter's hand was given with bittersweet emotion. Lance's next step was to enlist the help of Elizabeth's brothers, Matthew and Daniel, who agreed and sought assistance from their fellow police officers. No one could have guessed the extremes that were taken for this proposal to happen.

School had been in session for a week. Things were going well so far. Amy had a few unruly students which had been quite different than the previous year and she was struggling a little bit with learning to manage them effectively. Lance and Elizabeth as well as other colleagues offered suggestions and each day got better for Amy. Lance had been assigned to a new grade level and was adjusting well to it and his new team. Elizabeth was having a status quo kind of year, nothing different or new other than the faces in the desks.

She woke up the morning of her and Lance's one year anniversary with a smile on her face and joy in her heart. She looked around her townhouse and thought about how lucky she was to be where she was at this stage of her life. She seemed to have it all, a place of her own, a good career, a boyfriend most girls would die for, and a growing friendship with Amy.

Poor Amy, still living at home with her parents, had mentioned several times in the past year that she'd like to move out which Elizabeth took as hints to move in with her but that wasn't going to happen. Elizabeth loved her freedom in her little townhouse. Two bedrooms, yes, but she didn't want a roommate. Unless it would be Lance…she'd thought about asking him to move in and was sure he'd accept but it just hadn't come up yet. She'd already given him a key to her place but he only used it when she knew he was coming. She'd wait until he initiated the conversation about moving in together. They couldn't move into his little place, it was too small, too dark, not a place Elizabeth would be happy living in so if they decided to cohabitate it would have to be in Elizabeth's place. Plus, she owned, he rented.

Things were going wonderfully between them and he told her he had a special event planned for them that night. She had prodded for days for information, just a hint, as to what they were doing but he wouldn't offer a single word. When she had asked, "How should I dress?" hoping for some insight into whether they were going glamorous or casual, he responded, "yes." He wouldn't give her an inch and it was killing her. She was so used to being in control, having the upper hand but dating Lance had taken this role away from her on numerous occasions and she was learning that she didn't really mind.

She flipped through the dresses in her closet. Where was the white drop-waist dress that would look so good on her with her current bronzed color? Her tan looked gorgeous thanks to a last minute getaway to the beach right before in-service. Elizabeth loved the sun, loved to be tanned, it made her feel beautiful and happy and she secretly loved it when others commented on her tan. She hadn't worn the white dress in awhile and was in the mood for it. It was a little sexier than something she would normally wear to work but she was feeling really good about the day and figured it would be ok. She ran her fingers across the rims of the hangers two or three times, each time coming up with no white drop-waist dress. Where was it? She never let anyone borrow her clothing so that wasn't it.

She ran to the laundry basket and after rifling through to the bottom, found nothing. She hadn't expected to, the dress was dry clean only. Oh, had she taken it to the dry cleaner and forgotten to pick it up? That must be it, she thought, and made a mental note to pick it up soon. Returning to her bedroom and reaching back into her closet she selected a dress that was teacher-casual and grabbed a pair of flat strappy sandals to go with it. She knew she'd be coming home to change before going out with Lance so she wasn't very worried about her attire, it's just that the white drop-waist dress would have looked so good today, this being such a special day. Oh well, she thought, as she quickly dressed and finished the rest of the morning bathroom routine, I still look good.

Her thoughts again moved to the evening, what in the world could Lance be planning for their special evening? Elizabeth grabbed a bottle of juice and an untoasted bagel and ran out the door. If she'd had time she would've toasted it and added cream cheese but she was running late after spending time looking for the white dress. She slung her purse over her shoulder, grabbed her teacher bag that almost every teacher seemed to tote back and forth each day, and ran out the door to her car.

As she hit the unlock button on her key chain she realized once again how lucky she was to be where she was in life right now. She had heard her mother telling her father recently that one of her brothers was in constant battle with his wife over something that had to do with one of their kids. She sympathized with her brother, his wife could be a tough one but was thankful she wasn't in that position. Really, arguing over kids? One more reason not to have any, you couldn't fight over something you didn't have. She put the car in gear and headed off to work. Careful with the speed, she reminded herself, the Camaro had a lot of it and she needed to control it. Her brothers had threatened her within an inch of her life that if she ever got into trouble with the law for speeding, their names had better be the last ones she mentioned. They were upstanding and respected officers of the law but deep down she believed that if she got into trouble, they'd be there for her. She just thought they didn't want her depending on it and taking advantage, thus the threats.

Her path to work was straight through town. Eight blocks down the main thoroughfare and she was there. The weather was nice, warm but not hot or sticky and her window was down a pinch, not too much to mess her hair but enough to get some fresh air circulating. The lights all seemed to be in her favor today, green, green, green, a few more and if they all cooperated this well she might even get to work a few minutes early.

As she approached the square, the main intersection of her little town, she saw the familiar landmarks on the four corners, the court house, a church, a historical museum, and a small park. As she moved toward the traffic light she heard herself chanting, "stay green, stay green" and was glad there was no one to hear her being so silly. But the light did not cooperate, the green hue turned to yellow before she reached it. Just as the light turned yellow, it dawned on Elizabeth that there was no other traffic on the normally crowded streets that intersected the square. She hadn't noticed it before but indeed, hers was the only car on the street.

The next few minutes were a blur to Elizabeth. As she tried to figure out why there wasn't any traffic, the light turned red and she coasted to a stop at the base of the intersection. Within seconds police cars careened into the intersection from hidden sites on each of the four corners of the square. Had she had time to think she would have been panicked, but instead she was bewildered, confused, lost, and curious wondering what all of the excitement was about.

The police cars, with lights flashing and sirens blaring, proceeded to surround her car with their headlights pointed toward her so that indeed, her car was in the center of a circle of eight police cars. The irony, which she failed to realize at the moment, was that she was clearly at the center of everything right now, a position she loved in most of life's situations. Still shocked and unable to think, she watched as the door of the police car closest to her own car door opened.

Her eyes glanced around, were her brothers here? Whatever was happening was obviously a mistake and they'd help get it straightened out. Reality sank in and she felt a pang of fear rising in her. Before she could rationalize how to react to it, she saw someone getting out of the passenger side of one of the police cars. It was a man. Not a policeman though. She squinted her eyes and shielded them from the glare of the sun. He looked familiar, in fact he looked like Lance, but that was ridiculous, Lance came from the other end of town and would have already been at work by now and most importantly why in God's name would Lance be in a police car, one of which was surrounding her this morning on the square?

But it was Lance, she could tell now as he stood straight and tall. Even from the distance she recognized his smile, his dark eyes glistening in the sunshine, his handsome and tall body looming in the morning air. But why? The sirens stopped but the lights continued flashing. She reached for the handle of

47

the car just as Lance moved his hand to his mouth. What was in his hand?

"ELIZABETH MORRISON" came a booming voice that sounded like Lance. Why was it so loud? Oh my God he had the police car's radio in his hand and was depressing the loud-speaker button. But why? What was going on? "EIZABETH MORRISON" his voice boomed again, "PLEASE EXIT THE VEHICLE." Elizabeth's hand had reached the car door handle earlier and for the past few seconds she'd been frozen in place but now she lifted the handle and slowly opened it and began to exit the vehicle. Nothing else moved. No one else got out of cars. She looked around, still in shock and bewildered beyond belief, and closed her car door.

"ELIZABETH MORRISON, I HAVE LOVED YOU SINCE THE DAY I MET YOU, ONE YEAR AGO TODAY," Lance's voice boomed. Her feet were slowly moving toward him, she didn't know how, she wasn't making them move, but they were, they were moving right toward Lance. "ELIZABETH, MY LIFE WAS NOT NOR WILL IT EVER BE COMPLETE WITHOUT YOU IN IT AND I WANT THE WHOLE WORLD TO KNOW IT."

And then it hit her. Oh my God, he's proposing. He's proposing! "IF YOU WILL DO ME THE HONOR OF BECOMING MY WIFE, YOU WILL MAKE ME THE HAPPIEST MAN IN THE WORLD." By now Elizabeth was close enough to him that she could see the intricate features of his face, the features she'd grown to love so much, and she realized that at some point tears had begun falling down her cheeks. She looked straight into Lance's eyes and she saw happiness, love, and fear. She supposed he was scared of what her answer would be, and she realized that loving him meant making sure he was never afraid of losing her.

Lance dropped to one knee and magically, somehow, while she was engulfed in his handsome looks, a jeweler's box had replaced the police car radio in his hand. He reached out to her and took her left hand, asking, "Elizabeth, will you marry me?" Despite the flashing lights and the fact that there were at least eight police officers watching this happening right now, her mind and thoughts were completely focused on Lance. Their future danced before her eyes, just the two of them together, forever, and without a second's hesitation she said yes. Yes to her lifetime.

Lance rose to his feet and they simultaneously reached for each other in an embrace and kissed as tears of joy streamed down both their faces. Although it didn't distract her, the sound of a car door opening caught her attention followed by another familiar voice, her brother Daniel. "I take it you said yes, sis?"

Lance and Elizabeth turned to look at him and slowly, other police officers began exiting their vehicles. Smiling, she choked back what by now were sobs of happiness, looking around at all the police officers and townsfolk who had gathered for the excitement and yelled back, "Yes, I said yes!" as Lance pumped his fist into the air.

Out of the corner of her eye she saw someone approaching them; a female. It was Amy carrying a huge smile and a suitcase. It was obvious why she was here, she had been in on the plan all along but why did she have a suitcase? Where was she going?

Amy sat the suitcase down and ran to hug first Elizabeth and then Lance, and then all three sustained a long hug together with tear-stained faces. As Elizabeth pulled herself from the embrace, she looked quizzically at Amy as she realized the suitcase Amy had been carrying was actually one of her own, one from the set her parents had bought her for graduation. Amy blurted out more congratulations before Lance started to speak. "Elizabeth you are a hard person to surprise but I think we did it." He looked at Amy and they both nodded, slapping a high five, while Amy sniffed back the last few tears.

Lance continued. "We're going away now for the weekend, you and I, to celebrate." Elizabeth stood back, shocked, aware that the police officers and gathering townsfolk were still watching them, wondering what was being said amongst them.

"But, we have to go to work, I don't have anything with…" and then she realized what was in the suitcase. Apparently, using the key she had given him, Lance had gone into her townhouse Sunday while she was at the restaurant and packed a suitcase for her. This included, she would realize later, the white drop-waist dress she had been looking for just that morning. He had arranged for substitutes for both of their classes for the day and Amy was going to transfer Elizabeth's teacher bag on to school so that her sub would have what she needed for the day in the way of lesson plans. Everything had been taken care of, Elizabeth had absolutely no control whatsoever, and surprisingly, she couldn't be happier.

With a smile stretching from ear to ear Lance turned to the ever-growing crowd of spectators and announced loudly, "Ladies and Gentlemen, Elizabeth Morrison has just agreed to marry me and has made me the happiest man in the world," and he leaned down to kiss her. With that, everyone began clapping and cheering, joined by police officers as both of Elizabeth's brothers came over to hug and congratulate them and offer their congratulations. Police officers began getting back into their cars preparing to leave and restore the square to the public but first their sirens were turned back on while lights continued to flash helping to celebrate the couple's big moment. The whole event took less than two minutes. From here the plan was for Daniel to take Elizabeth's car home and Amy to drive Elizabeth and Lance back to Lance's truck which was at the police station. Amy would continue on to work and the newly engaged couple would leave for the weekend. What a morning it had been.

Chapter Four

"There is nothing on this earth more to be prized than true friendship." -Thomas Aquinas

Between Amy and her mother, Elizabeth didn't know which one was going to drive her to the brink of insanity first. Constantly hovering, calling regularly, all with the best of intentions but Elizabeth just wasn't used to other people involving themselves in her life. She knew they wanted to help, knew she needed them to help, but couldn't they be just a little less pushy? She caught herself snapping at each one of them, as well as at Lance a few times, out of sheer frustration. Amy had grown very close to her over the course of the eight months since the engagement. She had been slated for the maid of honor slot ever since the June wedding date was announced. Some of Elizabeth's friends whom she'd known longer were a little taken back by it but they didn't say anything, they were just happy to be a part of the ceremony.

In total she would have Amy and two additional bridesmaids plus her niece as a flower girl. One would think this should have been Elizabeth's choice but it wasn't, she didn't even want kids at her reception but her mother insisted that it would crush the child not to be a part of the ceremony. To keep the peace, Elizabeth agreed and as her mother expected, her niece was ecstatic. As for all the other conversations…flowers, dresses, food for the reception, invitations, guest lists, did it ever end? Elizabeth was enjoying these tasks to an extent but often found that she might have preferred to do them on her own without the sometimes critical input of her mother. If she had to hear, "Well at our wedding…" one more time, she thought she'd throw up. Her mother didn't get that no one cared about her wedding from so many years ago, this was all about Elizabeth now.

Amy had a disadvantage though. Her own family members always had an 'it doesn't matter what happens, we'll always be family' clause; however, she had to learn how to leave well enough alone when it was obvious Elizabeth knew what she wanted. And learn quickly she did. It was early on in the planning stages. Elizabeth and her bridal party were looking at gowns in a bridal store and of course each of the girls had their own opinion of what they ought to wear. They each selected several dresses and went to present them to Elizabeth. To each one that was displayed, Elizabeth would scrunch her nose and say no or wave it away with her hand until only one design remained on the rack. Of them all, it was the one Amy despised the most. But Elizabeth's mouth curled into a smile the moment she saw it and Amy knew she had to interject fast.

Before Amy could get a word out, Elizabeth proclaimed, "That's it! That's the dress! I love it! We can get Amy's in dark blue and Carrie and Lindsay's in light blue, that'll distinguish Amy as the maid of honor." This brought little pouts from Carrie and Lindsay that lasted only a second or two before Amy spoke up.

"Well Elizabeth I was thinking, what if I wore something completely different than they did? It could be in the same shade of blue as theirs and then all your colors would be the same in your pictures and I'd still be a little different."

Elizabeth turned and looked at her before asking, "What's wrong with *this* dress?"

"Nothing," Amy replied, "it's just that I'm not sure how it's going to look on me with my body shape." She was referring to her big boobs. "It'll look great on Lindsay and Carrie…" but she was interrupted before she could finish.

"It's going to look fabulous on all three of you Amy, no worries." And she turned and walked away while the three girls just looked at each other.

"Guess this is the dress," Amy said as she pulled out the skirt of it to take one more look. "And it is her special day so who cares how I'll look, right?" she added with a note of sarcasm. As they smirked, Lindsay and Carrie hoped Amy didn't notice. Welcome to the club, they thought.

Several months later all plans were complete, the big day was upon them and Elizabeth couldn't be happier. Things had really come together, due mostly in part to her mother and friends, whom she eventually acknowledged and thanked. Although she was nervous she had no doubts, no uncertainty, and no last minute cold feet to keep her from walking down the aisle. She was ready to become Mrs. Elizabeth Smith. She and Lance would live the life she'd always dreamed of, just the two of them, sleeping in on weekends, late night dinners, impulsive getaways; she was going to have it all with this wonderful man. And, as he told her very often, he was the lucky one to be getting her. She just knew the two of them would complete each other and they'd live the proverbial happily ever after. Once or twice Lance had mentioned having children but upon seeing Elizabeth's strange reaction to the topic, he wisely chose to end the conversations. He realized she was still young and they had plenty of time to start a family of their own so there was no reason to push her on it now.

Standing at the back of the Church with her father, Elizabeth found herself becoming nostalgic, thinking of days-gone-by and reliving some of the other happier moments of her life. She knew this one was the happiest of all and felt like the center of attention, as all brides should. Everyone was catering to her, most likely in an effort to keep her from going ballistic about something, but she was handling herself well. She only had to yell twice, once at the caterer who forgot to notate that there should be no green peppers in the salad and once at the florist who somehow managed to insert baby's breath in her bridesmaid's bouquets despite Elizabeth's directive that she didn't want any, anywhere. The thoughts that ran through her mind now seemed random but nonetheless, caused her to smile.

As she glanced over the back of her guest's heads, recognizing most of them even from the back, simple memories would pop into her mind and before she knew it she had tears rolling down her cheeks. Not one to usually notice emotions, her father surprised her by reaching his thumbs up under her eyes and swiping away the tears. "Hey, what's this?" The way her father whispered to her made her feel safe and cared for. "What's going on? Are you ok? Do you have cold feet?" More than likely the dollar signs were adding up before his eyes, she thought, he's worried that if the wedding is called off all his money will have gone to waste. No, on second thought, he seemed genuinely concerned as he eased a smile toward her. "You ok honey?"

She stifled back a slight sob and looked at him. "I'm fine Dad. I didn't think I'd get emotional like this. I'm confident in my decision to marry Lance, I know he is the best thing to ever happen to me and we're going to have a wonderful life. It's just that I seem to have gotten caught up in the moment."

Her dad smiled bigger then and reached down to hug her, careful not to mess her hair or makeup. "Lance is the lucky one honey. And before long you two will be adding to the family with grandchildren for us and…" Before he could finish, the organ music got louder which was their cue to begin the march down the aisle. Everyone stood and faced the back of the church where Elizabeth and her dad were poised. Smiles were on everyone's faces.

Those who knew Elizabeth well were a little shocked to see the startled look on her face when they saw her as she slowly proceeded down the aisle. They assumed the moment was just overwhelming and chalked it up to nerves. What they didn't know is that the only thing running through her mind were her father's last words to her seconds earlier, insinuating that Elizabeth would soon be the bearer of additions to the family's next generation.

"Gorgeous wedding, Elizabeth! The dresses, the flowers, the decorations, just perfect! But I doubt that anyone is surprised by that. You are such a lucky girl," said Robin as they chatted during the reception. Robin had been a reason in her life; she was the one who had sold Elizabeth the townhouse. The only reason she invited her to the wedding was because she had run into her about the time invitations were going out. When Elizabeth mentioned it, Robin said she couldn't wait to reply. Rather than hurt her feelings, Elizabeth just let it go and wrote out another invite. She suspected she'd never see Robin again after the wedding.

The reception hall had been decorated by her and her bridesmaids the night before and they had done a great job if she did say so herself. Everyone seemed to be enjoying themselves as she found herself separated from Lance for the first time. He was standing by the wall talking to a group of guys his age who she assumed were friends from high school or college. She'd walk over later and meet them but for now she was enjoying the few minutes of being able to relax her smile a little and not having to say thank you every other second for the extended congratulations.

Robin was chattering on about the wedding, her plans for her own wedding one day so could Elizabeth pass on the list of businesses she'd worked with, where were they going on the honeymoon, where were they going to live, would she still work when the babies start to come. Elizabeth had been letting Robin's voice drone on in her ear to avoid having to think or respond to anything just for a few seconds but that last one snapped her back to reality. Why was everyone insisting on talking about she and Lance starting a family today? For God's sake it was her wedding day. Surely people knew the purpose of a wedding wasn't to badger the bride to the point of frustration about a topic that really didn't lend itself to the wedding day. Elizabeth considered their decisions about children to be private, not to be discussed with anyone who chose to breech the topic on the happiest day of her life. She gave Robin a quick hug, thanked her for being there, and made an excuse to go meet Lance's friends.

As she approached the group of men, Lance reached for her with his arm. She settled into it and allowed him to introduce her to his friends who were indeed from his college days. They offered congratulations and told Elizabeth she was getting a good man but followed that with "do we ever have some stories to share." Knowing that she didn't care for this to happen now, Elizabeth thanked them for coming and asked if she could steal Lance away to meet some of her distant relatives who'd traveled for the wedding. She herself hadn't invited them or wanted them there, it had been her mother of course, but now they were opportune to get Elizabeth out of

58

listening to drunken college stories about her now-husband.

Glancing around the room Elizabeth found the long-lost relatives standing by her mother's table. Her mother and father had been seated with her brothers, their wives, and their children. Of all the tables in the room, that's the one Elizabeth's mom would want to be seated at, the one with the kids. Making her way to the table and pulling Lance behind her, she sucked in a deep breath and upon arrival, began the introductions. Pleasantries were exchanged and while Lance was busy telling her aunt how they'd met, one of Elizabeth's nephews got up from the table and came around to her. "Aunt Elizabeth you look very pretty." She leaned down to his level to hug him and say thanks. He himself looked very handsome in his rented tuxedo, she didn't realize they made them that small. As he leaned in to hug her she noticed the red juice mustache around his mouth but he'd turned his head to hug her so no harm done. She'd seen that before, the kid couldn't seem to get the juice in his mouth when he drank. Was it really that hard?

While he was hugging her, another of her young nephews got out of his seat and came around to join in the hug, this one around her waist and somewhat from behind. Now there were two of them hanging on to her neck and waist while she balanced on high heels in a squatting position. She tried to smile and look as the bride should when interacting with young children but it was difficult, she just wanted them to let go. She glanced up at her mother and Lance who were deep in conversation with her aunt and uncle; the topic seemed to have turned now to investments. Neither of them would be a help in rescuing her and Elizabeth needed her next get-away strategy now.

She reached down and unhooked the boys' arms from around her neck and waist and pushed them back a little in an effort to get up and make their excuses to move on. Apparently the boys weren't ready to separate and as Elizabeth tried to stand up, the boys latched back on to her. The imbalance of the two simultaneous movements resulted in Elizabeth being knocked off balance and toppling backwards with one boy trapped under her and one lying slightly askew on top of her. It didn't really cause much of a ruckus until the boys began howling with laughter, thinking this was the best thing to happen all day. People started looking and due to what they obviously considered the hilarity of it all, began pointing and chuckling which encouraged the boys to continue their own laughter. This made it harder for Elizabeth to push them off of her and regain her own composure.

Once Lance and her mother realized what was happening they scrambled to help her but not before the red-moustache bandit decided to plant a kiss on whatever was closest to him which, due to the fall, had been a spot below her left breast. As she stood and attempted to regain her composure, she saw her mother's gaze directed toward the spot as well as the look of horror on her face. Looking down, Elizabeth saw that she now had a small cherry-red mouth stain on her dress, visible to anyone who looked at her.

A mixture of emotions ran through her mind with anger topping the list, anger toward this little monster who ruined her dress, toward her mother for making her invite the kids when she didn't want them there in the first place, toward her brother and his wife for not teaching their kid better manners, and even toward Lance for having to discuss investments with her relatives instead of protecting her from the unforeseen incident.

All of a sudden everyone was surrounding her. Her sister-in-law was trying to get the kids, who were still carrying on with laughter, away from the situation, her mother was trying to dab at the stain with her bare hands, and Lance was standing nearby but unsure what to do. Only her relatives eased away, everyone else was still in the mix. Seeing the tears well in Elizabeth's eyes was enough for her mother and sister-in-law to know they had to act fast to avoid an explosion. Not knowing where he could best serve the situation, Lance backed up slightly and let the women take over.

Her sister-in-law handled the kids while her mother somehow managed to get hold of her arms and led her into a nearby bathroom. Once in the bathroom Elizabeth's words let loose along with more tears. Her wedding was ruined. The best day of her life, ruined. That's all she kept repeating as her mother tried to work the stain with a damp paper towel. This continued for several moments until the stain, albeit still evident, appeared somewhat lighter and Elizabeth seemed to have calmed down a little. Her mother wasn't sure if she had calmed down or wore herself out but either way, she had become quiet.

Her mother took the opportunity and eased Elizabeth into a chair. She knelt down in front of her daughter and sympathetically looked up into her eyes which were still red from the tears. "Elizabeth," she started, "your dad and I love you so much, and you were absolutely beautiful out there today. No one has ever been prouder than we were of you today." She reached up and brushed a strand of hair out of Elizabeth's face before continuing as Elizabeth just stared blankly. "You and Lance have something very special Elizabeth. You just had a beautiful ceremony before God and everyone who loves you where you vowed to love each other no matter what comes. That includes a silly little stain on your wedding dress on the most important day of your life. You may always remember what happened out there but most people won't and even if they do it doesn't matter. Lance is yours honey, he's yours for better or worse and with or without a Kool-Aid stain. He's your soul mate, just like daddy is mine. Elizabeth honey, he is your lifetime."

As she looked down at her mother she saw the slightest trace of tears in her eyes. She tried to recall having heart-to-heart conversations with her mother throughout the years and realized that she couldn't remember the last time it had happened. She felt her heart warm and then felt the tears spring back into her own eyes. Good Lord she had never cried so much in her life as she had today! She leaned down toward her mother and hugged her as tears flowed from both of them, tears of happiness. She hugged her hard and didn't let go for quite some time. She did love her mother, that was never a question, but in this moment she realized that perhaps her mother did actually serve more of a role in her life than what she had originally thought and as they hugged, she whispered her thanks to her mother.

Chapter Five

"Friends... they cherish one another's hopes. They are kind to one another's dreams." ~Henry David Thoreau

Fresh off the honeymoon, Elizabeth and Lance returned to their hometown in Central Pennsylvania as happy as ever. Having traveled to Cabo San Lucas, both had sun-kissed tans and looked healthy, vibrant, and glowing. Stopping in to visit friends and family, they shared pictures and stories of their adventures and answered questions and assured everyone who asked that no, she had not gotten pregnant during the honeymoon. People's nerve never ceased to amaze her.

The living arrangements had been decided before the wedding but no action had been taken. The options had been for Lance to move into the townhouse with Elizabeth, for Elizabeth to move into Lance's rental which she knew she couldn't do, or for them to buy or rent a place of their own. In the end the decision had been to rent a small cape cod in a neighboring town which was still close enough to family, friends, and work. The owners of the rental said they may consider a rent-to-own option and that had appealed to the young couple but they wanted to live in it first and see how they liked it. The area was clean, safe, and convenient to everything they'd need, they just wanted to see if it was a personal fit. The only thing they'd disagreed on was the number of bedrooms. Elizabeth thought two was plenty, one for them and one for guests but Lance was interested in more. As for Elizabeth's townhouse, Lance had suggested selling it and banking the money to use as a deposit when they were ready to buy but Elizabeth had another idea.

Elizabeth decided it was time to quit working at the Carriage House, after all she would be a married woman and she and her husband would have things to do on the weekends that didn't involve work and with both of them being teachers, they had a good two and a half months to enjoy each other before school started again. So she put her notice in much to the chagrin of the owners, they had come to realize what an asset she was to their business, and she had worked her last Sunday about three weeks before the wedding. When the rush slowed down and Elizabeth finally had a moment, she approached Amy. "Hey, how are things going at home with your parents?"

Rolling her eyes in typical Amy fashion, she said, "How do you think? You've been there, done that. It's always the same old thing, nag nag nag, do this, do that, don't put that there, this isn't where that goes, that's not how you do this, and on and on, it never ends. Thanks for reminding me how miserable I was though, I had nearly forgotten. You're such a good friend."

Elizabeth grinned and looked away to keep Amy from seeing the smirk on her face. "Yeah I remember, only too well. Which is why I have an offer you can't refuse."

Amy shifted her weight to her back foot, folded her arms and said, "I'm all ears." Elizabeth braced herself squarely in front of Amy and told her that she and Lance would be moving into a new house and that Lance had wanted her to sell the townhouse but deep down she wanted to keep it. It was something she had worked for, she had done it on her own, and she wasn't ready to let it go. She wanted to keep it as a rental unit and she wanted Amy to be the one to rent it. With each sentence Amy's smile and level of anticipation got bigger and bigger until finally she yelled, "Yes! I'll take it!"

Elizabeth immediately cut in. "I only want the amount of the mortgage as your rent, nothing extra. You pay all utilities and keep it in good shape and we'll both be happy. What do you say?"

Still smiling larger than life Amy screeched, "I already said yes! I don't care what you want to charge, I'll make it work! I love your townhouse and I need to be out of my parent's place. It's perfect. When can I move in? Is there room for all my stuff? Can I have a pet? Do you care if I still have people over after work on Sundays?"

She would have kept going with the questions if Elizabeth had not stopped her. "Whoa! Hold on Aim, we'll work all that out, I just wanted to make sure you were interested before I told Lance. I don't know how he'll feel about it but it doesn't really matter, it's mine and I can do what I want with it. So we have a deal."

"We do," Amy said smiling, nodding her head and extending her hand to shake. Elizabeth looked at her friend's hand and grabbed her into a hug, a big sisterly hug, and both girls laughed out loud at the excitement each was facing in their immediate future.

Equipped with friends and pick-up trucks, the entourage first moved all of Elizabeth's things to the new cape-cod and then they moved Amy's things from her parent's house into the townhouse. Amy didn't care that it wasn't cleaned in between the moves, she just wanted in and said she'd do all the cleaning herself. That suited Elizabeth just fine. The final move was to move the few things Lance had from his apartment to their new place. Little by little both parties settled in to their new living arrangements and both were quite happy. Elizabeth had her husband and new house, Amy had her freedom. What could be better? What more could either one want? Nothing, as far as Elizabeth was concerned.

As for Amy, she would have loved to have a special someone in her life and perhaps follow in Elizabeth's footsteps down the aisle but for now, there was no one. She'd had a date here and there but nothing ever panned out. Usually it was Amy who made the decision that it wasn't worth pursuing, she was having a hard time meeting a quality person. Either they didn't have a job or their job required them to travel six days a week or their job was not something conducive to the lifestyle of dating a school teacher (such as the guy who danced with an all-male review troupe). There was one that Amy felt was perfect in just about every way but there were some characteristics that made her believe he hadn't realized yet that he was gay. So for now she was enjoying single life in her new townhouse, parent-free. Elizabeth's life as a married woman was great.

At first they went out to eat dinner nearly every night and when Lance asked that Elizabeth start cooking at home sometimes, she did and found that she actually enjoyed it. She would call her mother for recipes and explanations of what unfamiliar cooking terms meant. She was actually enjoying these conversations with her mother and admitted to herself more than once that she had never envisioned doing so. She wasn't the best cook, both she and Lance agreed on that, but she was learning and was willing to try and that's what mattered. Lance really appreciated her efforts and let her know often by surprising her with flowers or small gifts. She kept a neat house, again not perfect but clean enough that Lance had no complaints. Their sex life had been good when they were dating and showed no signs of changing once they were married. This was a welcome relief to her as she had heard that once a couple marries, the sex life is the first thing to go. She could now respond to those comments that it just wasn't true.

They enjoyed spending time with their married friends. Sometimes those couples had kids and those were the ones Elizabeth tried to excuse her way out of but Lance usually won and they'd go. She just didn't enjoy it as much. Lance on the other hand could often be found in the playrooms or backyards interacting with the kids. Elizabeth would just wave it away with a flick of her wrist and tell their friends, "What can I say, he's a kid at heart."

Of course she had to endure their comments such as, "Wait till you have your own!" "Lance will be such a good dad!" "Look at him! He's a natural with kids!" And her all-time favorite, "You guys can borrow them for awhile if you want, you know." Sure, just what she wanted, someone else's kids at her house interfering with her life. Not!

School started again and the months went by quickly. All three friends were having a great year and Elizabeth and Lance were living the honeymoon life. For their first Christmas together, Lance gave Elizabeth a beautiful tennis bracelet. She wore it and showed it off to anyone who would look. She was so lucky to have this man all to herself.

A few weeks after the Christmas holidays, Lance and Elizabeth were invited to a Saturday night party by friends who had just had their first baby in November. The baby was at the party but was being taken care of by someone in the nursery and therefore not really present. That suited Elizabeth just fine. The last thing she needed was an interruption of their fun by a crying baby, a baby who would grow into a kid who would have a red juice mustache and ruin someone's wedding day. These particular friends had been friends of Elizabeth's and had met and welcomed

Lance into their circle long before now but they had never really socialized together much.

As Elizabeth chatted with the women about hairstyles, where the cheapest and longest-lasting manicures could be found, and about their husbands in general, she found herself engrossed in the conversation to the point that she didn't realize Lance had not been nearby for over an hour. When she did, she looked around and spotted the group of men she would have expected him to be talking to but found Lance absent. She walked into the kitchen where a small group of women were deciding how much rum to pour into the punchbowl to make it just right but no Lance. She glanced out the windows into the backyard, thinking it would be too cold to be out there and she was right, no Lance.

Not really worried but curious, she began moving through the halls, opening doors and peeking in to try and find her husband. On her way toward the stairs she nearly ran into a young girl of about 16 years who she didn't recognize. "Hi," Elizabeth said extending a hand, "I'm Elizabeth."

The girl shook her hand and introduced herself as the niece of the couple whose house they were in. She indicated that they were paying her to watch the baby during the party. Not very responsible, Elizabeth thought, leaving the baby alone somewhere while you're out here doing God knows what. Probably trying to find some leftover drinks to confiscate or something. She knew teens did that kind of thing. Elizabeth excused herself with a 'nice to meet you' and continued up the stairs to look for Lance.

The first room was the master bedroom and she quickly pulled the door shut upon realizing it. All of a sudden she felt like a spy, like she was snooping, like she shouldn't be there. But she was looking for her husband and she had every right to do that. The door to the second room was open. It was a bathroom and no Lance inside. The door adjacent to the bathroom was slightly ajar and Elizabeth walked over and gently pushed it open while she remained standing in the hallway.

She heard before she saw. She heard the faint sound of baby music, the tune she did not recognize but she knew it was lullaby-ish. She heard the murmuring of a soft voice, a man's voice, one she thought she recognized but had not heard in this particular tone before. And she heard the unmistakable sound of a baby cooing. Hesitantly she listened around the door and peeked behind it to see Lance sitting in a rocking chair by the window holding a pink bundle, talking to the bundle with a soft sing-song voice she had never heard him use while the musical mobile spun above the crib producing the soft music she'd heard.

The baby appeared to be gazing intently into Lance's eyes, cooing, as if responding to Lance's conversation in its own language. Certainly not the sight Elizabeth expected to see when she did locate her husband. She stood peering around the door staring at the two of them unsure if she should interrupt or not, it looked so private.

Before she could make a decision as to what she should do, the couple's niece walked through the door brushing slightly against Elizabeth. "I'm back," she said to Lance as if he should know where she had been and why she was gone. Lance looked up and saw her carrying a baby bottle and at the same time noticed Elizabeth standing in the doorway, somewhat shell-shocked. Startled, his expression turned blank as he rose and gently handed the baby back to the sitter and then walked toward Elizabeth.

"That's little Megan," he whispered to Elizabeth. "Isn't she just the most adorable thing you've ever seen?" She didn't know if she was supposed to answer that or not but her answer would have been no. Lance continued, "She's going to feed her now. Do you want to hold her?"

Shocked by the question, Elizabeth took a step backward. "No," she blurted out louder than she meant to and with no doubt and much emphasis. The sitter looked up to shush them as she rocked and fed the baby and Elizabeth took this as a cue to leave the room. Lance followed her out into the hall where they stood and stared at each other. Neither one understood why this was such an awkward moment but it was. Not knowing what else to do, Lance leaned in and kissed his wife and then took her hand and led her back to the party. Nothing more was said about the baby but Elizabeth knew that the time had come to have the discussion about their future without children.

Amy hadn't been invited to the party despite the fact that she knew the host and hostess. It had obviously been a couple's party and Amy wasn't part of a couple. Just as well, she had the first shift at the

Carriage House Sunday morning and would have to be in extra early. Setting her alarm and settling into her bed with a new novel she'd just purchased, it wasn't long before her eyelids were feeling heavy and she nodded off to sleep.

She awoke to the alarm, lights still on, her book having slipped from her hand, and a stiff neck. Slowly turning her neck from side to side, she got up and showered for work. As she finished drying off, she hoisted the towel to the rack and noticed a stain of bright red blood on it. Great, she thought, early morning shift, stiff neck, and now my period, what's next? She felt herself moving slower than usual and suspected she'd be a little late. Oh well, life happens.

Once ready for work, she left the townhouse en route for the Carriage House and arrived a few minutes late. Mark's truck was there, of course, and there was another car in the lot with no driver present which meant Mark had let the customer in and took his order. Great, she thought. She had established the same deal with him that Elizabeth had when she was the opening waitress. Mark would handle customers due to her lateness and he keeps the tip with her doubling it. On top of that, she'd have to deal with Mark harassing her for being late. She didn't have as close a relationship with him as Elizabeth had and she hoped to one day but for now, they got along ok. Whatever, she said to herself, add this to the type of day I'm going to have, she thought.

Entering the restaurant, Amy hung her purse on the hook in the back and walked into the kitchen, prepared for dialogue with Mark. She glanced at him

73

behind the line and mumbled a 'mornin' his way. His reply set the tone for the day. "You're late, I took the first order, and he's a Lieutenant with the Army so get ready to double." They all knew the officers tipped well regardless of their rank. Amy cursed the curse that made her late and headed toward the front.

The sound of bacon sizzling made her hungry and she was already looking forward to her break. She wondered what Mark's specials were today, she had to admit the man could cook. As she pushed the swinging door open into the restaurant, she scanned the area for her, well, Mark's customer and saw no one. She stopped and turned back toward the kitchen, about to ask Mark where he went when she heard the bathroom door open. Ah, she hadn't thought of that, he was washing up for breakfast. At least he's clean, she thought.

As Amy approached the floor again she wasn't prepared for what she encountered emerging from the bathroom. This man was at least 6'5", the traditional military haircut, and very handsome wearing what she knew were called ACUs. She didn't know what the acronym stood for but she knew it was what they called their everyday uniform. She wasn't one to be drawn to men in uniform like some girls she knew but she sure was to this one. Wow, she hadn't seen a man this good looking in a long time. She noticed the rank on his uniform but had Mark not told her, she wouldn't have known he was a Lieutenant, she didn't know what the different symbols meant. His eyes caught hers, oh man, gorgeous brown eyes to boot, I'm in love, she thought. Both smiled at the same time.

"Good morning, sir." Amy said. She had learned that respect for officers was expected by her bosses, they were trying to forge a bigger working relationship with the Army base and knew their employees could enhance the chances of it happening through their interaction with the soldiers.

"Good morning mam," he replied. They both smiled at each other simultaneously as they spoke. There was an awkward period of silence when neither one said anything; he broke it first. "You sure are better looking than the guy who got my coffee and took my order."

Feeling suddenly shy, Amy blushed a little. "Thanks," she said, "that's Mark, he helps when he can. Does your coffee need to be refilled?" The usual talk between a waitress and a customer, how invigorating. She headed toward the coffee station and grabbed the pot to refill the soldier's cup.

"Sure, he said, and how about an OJ?" Anything for you, Amy thought. As she poured his juice she heard the clang of the bell on the front door, another customer, dang it, there goes our alone time. She almost laughed out loud at her silly thought. This man was most likely married, with kids, and not at all interested in her.

She proceeded to take care of her other customers while Mark served the Lieutenant his breakfast-this was part of the deal, if Mark was going to take the tip he had to follow through with the service. He had ordered one of the specials - Huevos Rancheros - an uncommon but popular Mexican dish in the area. It was a huge plate and Amy never knew how anyone could eat it all, in fact most people didn't finish it. By the time he was halfway through it she'd gotten about five more tables and she was busy bustling around the restaurant, taking orders, refilling coffees.

She nearly forgot the Lieutenant until she passed his table and noticed the plate was empty. Holy cow, so much food, but then again this man was a big man and so she supposed it made sense that he could eat the whole meal. "How was it?" she asked.

His response made her laugh, "It was terrible and I ate it all to make sure." They made eye contact again, were those butterflies she felt? Surely not. As she reached to take his plate, she scanned his left hand. No ring! Still not a clear sign but she could remain hopeful.

"So why are you here so early on a Sunday morning, in your work clothes no less?" she asked him. He explained that he was flying out to attend a training which would prepare him for a deployment to Afghanistan. Mark came out just then to finish up his one and only customer but Amy shot him 'the look.' Having four sisters and a wife, Mark knew 'the look'. He came to a halt and backed his way back into the kitchen. Amy pulled her waitress pad out and began to prepare a check for him. As she wrote, she could have sworn she saw him glance at *her* left hand which, of course, was bare. She placed the check face down on the table and started to tell him he could pay at the register but he began speaking at the same time.

"My name's Mike," and Amy introduced herself. For a moment she felt like they were the only two in the restaurant. All her other customers were taken care of though so she didn't need to worry. They made a little more small talk until Mike glanced at his watch and indicated he'd have to get moving to catch his flight. He asked if he could leave his money with the check on the table. Of course, Amy told him as she smiled and walked away. With that, Mike stood, all 6'5 of him, and left.

There he goes she thought, the man of my dreams. Handsome, polite, and I'll probably never see him again but as he exited more customers entered. Time to get back to reality, she thought as she hurried from table to table and customer to customer, gosh it was busy, she nearly forgot to clear Mike's table until she saw a couple at the door looking for an empty one. Normally the clean up would have been Mark's duty but 'the look' exempted him from further duty so Amy quickly went to it and began to clear it for other customers.

As she grabbed his check, which had totaled $8.57, she was shocked beyond belief to find a twenty dollar bill lying atop the check. Normally her first thought would've been, crap, this all goes to Mark and I have to double it. Her thought right now, however, was, he must like me to have left me this much tip! She took the check and the twenty to the check-out counter and after ringing it in, she turned it over to validate it through the register and there on the back was a note, it said, "I will be back in town on Friday, I'd like to take you out for dinner, please call me if you're interested. If you don't call, I won't ever be able to show my face in here again and that would be a shame because the

Huevos Rancheros are the best ever. Mike" and a phone number was included.

Amy was so giddy she couldn't help the nervous giggles that escaped her mouth. She pocketed the tip, to hell with Mark, and greeted the next customers at the door. Then she proceeded to have the happiest work day she'd ever had at the Carriage House. Other than Mike, her only thoughts were that she couldn't wait to tell Elizabeth.

Chapter Six

"Love is blind; friendship closes its eyes."
  -Friedrich Nietzsche

Elizabeth was on the recliner in the living room, curled up in a blanket, eating popcorn and watching Lifetime. For most this would be an ideal way to spend a lazy Sunday but Elizabeth was not enjoying the leisure time. She grabbed the remote and was about to channel surf when the phone rang, it was Amy. It didn't take long for Amy to notice that something was wrong by listening to Elizabeth's voice. She asked if she could come over, her reason was now two-fold; she could find out what was bothering Elizabeth *and* share her news of an upcoming date. Elizabeth said sure and hung up.

      She wasn't really up for company but she also wasn't in the mood to think of an excuse. She couldn't shake the feeling she was having. After finding Lance with the baby at the party last night, she realized how intent he was on having children and felt more pressure than ever to consider pregnancy in the near future. She didn't mention it to him, she didn't bring it up at all, but as soon as they left the party the thoughts infiltrated her mind. Absorbed in her own mind, she'd barely spoken to Lance since they left the party and when it continued into the morning and Lance tried to find out what was bothering her, to no avail, he'd said he'd had enough and he left to visit her brother's family. He'd grown very close to both of her brothers but particularly to Daniel. Daniel's family was the Norman Rockwell family. Daniel himself was very family oriented, they never did anything unless it was as a family. Elizabeth remembered the time her mother wanted Daniel's wife to go on a weekend shopping spree with her and she declined the invitation. A little hurt, her mother had called Daniel to find out if she'd upset his wife but Daniel told her no, they simply don't do anything unless it's together. Elizabeth had thought that was the most ridiculous thing she'd ever heard of but nonetheless, Lance sure seemed to like spending time with them.

Amy made the short trip to the neighboring town and arrived at Elizabeth's doorstep with a smile from ear to ear. She was shocked to see Elizabeth's appearance and her smile immediately turned to a look of concern. "What's wrong? Are you sick? Is it Lance? Is he sick?" Amy continued pummeling her with questions as she pushed her way into the house. Elizabeth went to the couch, Amy joined her, and Elizabeth shared what was bothering her and told her about the situation in the baby's room at the party the previous night. Other than the pregnancy scare she had never really had problems before, never needed a friend to lean on, and she found herself in a very comfortable position with Amy and didn't hold back her feelings.

Amy listened intently. "Don't you think you'll ever want kids, Elizabeth? I mean, you seem to get along with your niece and nephews just fine, and you always tolerated Gina's kids at the Carriage House parties, and you're a teacher for crying out loud."

Even as Amy was speaking, Elizabeth was shaking her head. "I can't say never but it's nothing I want anytime soon and even then I can't guarantee I'll ever want kids. If it were up to Lance we'd be pregnant by now. What if five years go by and we have none, will he be happy? What if I agree to go ahead and have one, will I be happy? It just doesn't seem like there's an easy answer," Elizabeth said as tears filled her eyes.

Amy knew this was serious, Elizabeth was not a crier. In the back of her mind Amy had to wonder if they hadn't talked about this before marriage but she didn't dare bring that up now. The friends discussed it a little further until Amy finally said, "Elizabeth you're going to have to discuss this with Lance. That's the only way. You know what you want, he knows what he wants, and you both know when, where, and how you're willing to give. You know better than I do that marriage is about give and take."

But Elizabeth didn't think she did know that, she hadn't had to give on anything in their marriage thus far. Sure it hadn't been quite a year yet but Lance was always the one to give in, always the one to compromise, but she wasn't so sure he would on this one. They talked a little more and then Amy remembered her initial reason for wanting to come over. She wanted to be careful though, she didn't want Elizabeth to think she wasn't concerned about her problem, she wanted to be there for her friend.

"Elizabeth, is there anything else you want to talk about? Anything more I can say or do? I mean, like I said, this is really a discussion you and Lance need to have."

"I know," Elizabeth said, "I know. And I will. I'll talk to him when he gets home. He's at Daniel's right now." She got up for a tissue and blew her nose. "I can't believe I'm this upset about the whole thing. And he has no idea why I'm upset. I just kind of ignored him because I didn't know what to say." Amy stood up and hugged her friend.

"Talk to him Elizabeth, you two can work this out. Talk to him." As they both sat back down Amy continued, "And besides, I have some good news to share, do you want to hear it?" Elizabeth smiled, which allowed Amy to feel comfortable smiling, and then she spilled her story.

Excitement eluded from her as she spoke, Elizabeth could not remember ever seeing her like this and she was genuinely happy for her friend. Being the forever pessimist though, she cautioned Amy, "Just relax a little Aim, you haven't even gone out with him yet. He could turn out to be a dud like the others." They both laughed and recalled some of the duds she'd dated in the past which resulted in more laughter. Amy was glad to see her friend laughing.

"I have a week to wait Elizabeth, it's going to seem like forever but I'm so excited. There was just something about him, I can't explain it."

82

And then she told her about the tip. "Holy shit Aim, he's in love!" They both laughed at that.

The girls sat and chatted a little while longer until Lance walked in the front door. Beaming with excitement he didn't even acknowledge Amy, he just blurted out, "Daniel and Vanessa are pregnant again!"

Their faces fell a little and Amy stood. "Hi Lance," she said, "That's great, please share my congrats with them. I was just leaving." She glanced back at Elizabeth with a concerned look and mouthed the words 'talk to him' as Lance quickly hugged Amy and then went to join his wife on the couch. He put his arm around Elizabeth's shoulders.

"Isn't this great hon? They were asking if we were maybe thinking of getting pregnant soon too and how cool it would be for the kids to have cousins their age..." His voice droned off as Amy quietly slipped out the front door leaving Elizabeth on the couch with a terrorized look on her face.

The conversation with Lance didn't go well at all. Naturally he could tell something was wrong. His first thought was that his wife may already be pregnant, thus the moodiness, and he expressed this to her. "No Lance, I'm not pregnant, there's no chance at all that I'm pregnant." He nuzzled a little closer to her, kissing her lightly on the lips.

"Well nothing says we can't go try right now, does it?" he whispered into her ear. With that Elizabeth broke down in tears which turned to sobs. At a total loss for words, Lance just sat and stared at his wife. When she regained her composure and was able to talk, she told him. She told him everything. She told

83

him that she'd never really thought about kids that much, that she never saw herself as a mother, and that the thought of kids holding her back from doing anything she wanted made her angry. She even said she was worried about the physical pain of childbirth, she'd heard horror stories. She told him that whenever he mentioned kids during their dating period, she just let him talk and figured he'd get over it. She almost brought up the incident with her nephew from the wedding to point out how kids ruin everything but even she knew that would make her sound juvenile. She ended the speech bluntly. "I just don't know if I will ever want kids of my own."

Now Lance's face looked fallen. He looked as if he'd just lost everything that ever meant anything to him. "Elizabeth I love you, and I know you love me, and to have a baby together would be a result of that love. How can you not want that? Don't you have a, what do they call it, a maternal instinct or something like that?"

He looked at her hopefully as her tears began to return. "I don't know Lance. I don't know. It's just not something I want for myself."

With that Lance stood up and he surprised himself with the way he spoke to his wife. "For yourself? For yourself?" he screamed at her. "What about me? And more importantly, what about us? Huh? What about us? We're married, Elizabeth," he yelled, pointing at his ring. "Don't you think I should have a say in this? Why is it always about you and what you want? You know Elizabeth I never considered you to be spoiled or self-centered or anything like that but right now I'm seeing a side of you I never knew existed. You're thinking only of yourself."

The speech seemed to go on forever in Elizabeth's ears. She was hearing everything he was saying and she couldn't say she disagreed completely, but she also couldn't bring herself to give in. Lance finally retreated to their bedroom and slammed the door, leaving his wife crying on the couch. She buried her face in a pillow and cried like she never cried before, trying to figure out what in the world had happened in the past 24 hours to make her life turn so upside down.

For Amy the week drug on. She couldn't believe her excitement as Friday lurked closer and closer each day. She was cautious not to mention it to Elizabeth and Elizabeth, wrapped up in her own problems, didn't bring it up either. In that the three still taught together in the same building, the tension between the husband and wife was obvious and it was felt by anyone who associated with them both. Lance hadn't mentioned anything to Amy, he probably assumed she was Elizabeth's confidant, which was fine, but it left him with no one to talk to about the situation. Not that he would've anyway. He didn't want to involve Elizabeth's family either. Deep down he thought she'd come around, just as she thought he would, but both could not have been more wrong. It seemed their marriage was bearing its first true test. The problem was, neither of them knew how they could move past this if neither one was willing to give.

Thursday afternoon found the three sitting together at an after-school faculty meeting. Amy felt uncomfortable but tried to keep the conversation light to avoid the deafening silence that ensued otherwise. The meeting hadn't started yet so she said, "You guys have plans this weekend?" hoping it may spark Elizabeth's memory of Amy's own impending plans. Both shook their head but didn't utter a word. "Any good movies out there you guys want to see?" she asked. Again, two heads shaking.

She was just about to give up when Elizabeth spoke. "I think I'm going to the beach." Both Lance and Amy startled a little at the statement. Almost simultaneously, Amy said, "But it's cold out, the beach won't be any fun," while Lance said, "When were you going to tell me about this?"

Elizabeth looked first at Amy and then at Lance. She stood up and said to Lance, "We'll talk about it tonight at home." And with that she headed toward the door. Lance and Amy just stared at each other in disbelief. They watched as Elizabeth stopped and spoke to their principal, obviously feigning an excuse, and then walked out of the room.

That evening at the Smith house was a nightmare. Lance walked in the door to find Elizabeth sitting at the kitchen table. He could tell she'd been crying by the tissues on the table and the redness in her eyes. He wasn't sure what to say so he just sat down beside her and looked at her. She looked up at him and for no reason at all she asked him, "Did I miss

86

anything at the faculty meeting?" Lance shook his head.

"What's happening to us Elizabeth?" he asked her. "Last weekend we left for a party and everything was fine, less than a week later and we aren't talking, we aren't making love, we aren't even acknowledging each other's presence when we're in a room together." This pooled more tears in Elizabeth's eyes. She looked as if she was struggling to gain her composure but to no avail, so she just started to speak.

"Lance, I'm sorry. I'm so sorry. Baby I do love you, you know that, with all my heart I love you, but the bottom line is I do not want to have children. Not now, not next year, probably not ever. I don't see my mind changing on this. I've thought about it long and hard Lance, I have, and this is what I've come to. No kids for me. The only question left for you is, can you stay married to me and live with that? Can you agree to not having children? Can you be happy with just me, only me, for the rest of your life?" She stopped talking and realized that somewhere in the middle of her words, Lance had hung his head down and wrapped his hands around the back of his neck.

He sat like this for what seemed like an eternity. He loved Elizabeth but the compromise she was asking him to make seemed to cause his heart physical pain. When he finally raised his head, his eyes were red. He looked around the kitchen. At the refrigerator. At the stove. At the dishwasher. At the sink. At anything to avoid looking at Elizabeth. Sensing the avoidance and feeling as if he may be ready to concede, Elizabeth stood and walked to her husband. She stood behind him, arms draped over the front of him, and kissed his head. She moved herself around to the side of him and knelt down, putting herself below his eye level. She put her hand on his leg, using her other hand to cup his chin and pull the direction of his head, and therefore his eyes, downward toward hers. Their eyes made contact and stayed connected for what seemed like forever.

Elizabeth was eager yet anxious to hear his response and although she was feeling pretty confident she knew the answer, there was a part of her that realized she may be wrong. Lance took Elizabeth's hand from his chin and ever so gently raised it to his lips. He kissed her hand, inhaled deeply before exhaling, and said one word.

"No."

The word hung in the air as tears streamed down Lance's face. Lance stood from the chair, raising Elizabeth back to a standing position with him, and hugged her tightly. Not quite sure what he was saying no to, Elizabeth stood and allowed herself to be hugged with a confused look on her face. Lance held her tightly but she managed to pull back from him.

Searching his face for answers and finding none that she could interpret, she asked him, "No, what?"

He stood back, wiping his eyes once again and shaking his head. "No to all that you asked Elizabeth. I want kids, you've known that since before we got married, and I love you more than life itself but giving up kids is not something I can do. If that means I have to give you up, as hard as it will be, and as much as I don't want to, then that's what I have to do. Hell Elizabeth I'd even be willing to wait a few more years until you're ready, but you said you can't guarantee you'll want them even then. That's not a chance I can take babe, I want a family of my own and that includes kids. Period."

Now it was Elizabeth's turn to be shocked. She didn't expect to hear that he'd be willing to give her up so easily and not compromise with her, she wasn't realizing that she, on the other hand, was not compromising with him but in this situation, there didn't seem to be a viable compromise. For an instant she felt rejected, as if he was choosing kids over her, and in reality he was, kids he didn't even know yet. For all they knew they might not be able to conceive, then what? How could he throw their love away like that?

Elizabeth turned and walked away, stunned and not knowing what to say. She headed toward the bedroom and Lance let her go. She lay on the bed, tearing up just a little but more in shock than anything. It was unbelievable, less than a week after their first real fight and her marriage was over. She lay there in the quiet for hours while outside, light turned to dark and the neon numbers on her clock ticked away the minutes of the day, of her life, and all she could do was lay there.

When she finally stood from the bed, it was almost midnight. Both she and Lance had to teach the next day so she thought it was probably best to go tell him to come to bed so they could get some sleep, she wondered if he'd fallen asleep on the couch already. As she walked out into the living room it was pitch dark, no lights were on, nor did she hear the background noise of the television. She flicked the overhead light of the living room on and visually scanned the room, only to find it empty. She walked to the kitchen, same thing. Assuming Lance went into the guest bedroom, she walked towards it to tell him to come to their bed. She didn't know if she was doing the right thing or not, she'd never been in this position before, but they were a married couple and surely it was fine for them to share a bed at night despite the fact that their marriage was in trouble.

She knocked gently. "Lance," she called out as she pushed the door open, "come on to bed," and she turned the overhead light on. But the bed was empty. Somewhat shocked, she ran to the front door and pulled it open. Looking out onto the street, she saw her Camaro and nothing else, certainly not the Ford F250 that her husband drove. Quite simply put, Lance was gone. Elizabeth's unwillingness to compromise on the idea of bringing children into the world had resulted in the death of her marriage.

Amy was up at the crack of dawn Friday morning, this was the day she'd been waiting for. Mike's number was posted on her corkboard by the kitchen phone. She'd also entered it into her cell in the event the paper was misplaced. She wasn't taking any chances. If she lost the number he would assume she didn't want to see him, and if that happened he'd already said he wouldn't come back into the restaurant and thus she'd never see him again. She couldn't let that happen.

She wondered what time she should call, he hadn't said, and she wanted to call right then and there, she was just that excited. Sure it was 6 AM but it was Friday, the day he said to call, and didn't Army people get up early anyway for PT? He was probably up. But what if he's flying, then she'd get his voice mail and he'd think, gosh, she couldn't even wait till I landed. No, calling now was not the answer. She would wait until after school. At least she'd try to wait until after school. She had a 45-minute planning period at 10:00 AM when she could make the call and a 30-minute lunch period that was her time to do as she wished, so if the waiting got the better of her she might just make the call during one of those times.

Amy got ready for work and headed in. She thought briefly about Lance and Elizabeth and wondered how they made out the night before, she was sure they'd work it out one way or the other but she also realized the seriousness of the conflict. It was a biggie for sure. For a fleeting moment she thought about having kids with Mike then quickly realized how foolish she sounded to herself and tried to occupy her mind with work-related things. To no avail. Her mind wandered back to Mike time and time again. What kind of hold did this man have on her, she wondered? She'd only known him for an hour at best!

Amy's morning went well. She had several students absent with the flu, one of which was one of her least favorite kids. While she hated to admit it, there always seemed to be one you didn't care for as much as the others and this kid was 'the one' this year. It also seemed that these kids never got sick, they were always present, but this one had gotten the flu so he'd been out for most of the week. She hadn't seen Lance or Elizabeth that morning in the faculty room but she hadn't had time to run to their rooms. She figured she'd check in with her friends during her planning period. She reassured herself that they'd be ok, they had a strong marriage and most times she was envious. There were times she was thankful she was single but most times she wanted the white picket fence deal.

The hands on the clock in her classroom seemed to be creeping their way around the face of it today and it seemed like forever until it was time for her planning period. She dropped her kids off in the gym and pulled her cell phone out of her pocket. This was the test, would she call him now or would she be able to make herself wait? Glancing at the phone she realized she'd missed a call. The caller had left a voice message though. For an instant she thought, what if it was Mike? But then she remembered he didn't have her number, instead, she had his. She punched in the code to retrieve the voice message and was surprised to hear the voice of her boss from the Carriage House.

"Hi Amy, its Jerry from the Carriage House. I'm sorry to bother you but you have a beautiful floral arrangement waiting for you here, it was delivered early this morning and I know you aren't scheduled to work again until Sunday. They're too beautiful not to enjoy so I thought I'd give you a call, maybe you can swing by and pick them up after school today? Of course if you don't want them, they do look very nice sitting here on the counter…See you soon."

Amy didn't realize it until she hung up but a smile had erupted on her face as she listened to the message. Flowers? For her? From who? She had no idea. It wasn't anywhere near her birthday and Valentine's Day was weeks away, not that anyone would send her flowers for Valentine's Day. And then it hit her, what if Mike had sent them? He knew she worked there and had no way of knowing she only worked there on Sundays during the school year. He didn't even know she was a teacher! They had to be from him. Oh but what if they weren't? She didn't want to get her hopes up but it was killing her.

Forgetting all about Elizabeth and Lance, she ran to the office and startled the secretary with her sudden entrance. "Barb, I have a slight emergency, I have to run a personal errand and I know we're not supposed to do that during our planning time but I really need to just this once. Do you think the boss will mind?" Barb kept her fingers pressed to her keyboard keys as she tilted her head toward the principal's office. "He's in there, go ahead on in and ask him." Amy popped in, interrupted politely, and reiterated the request. Her boss was a very reasonable man. He was fair, she liked that, and he didn't play favorites. He seemed genuinely interested in the success of his students and Amy found that impressive since she'd always thought principals were just PR people.

Permission granted, she grabbed her purse and keys and flew out the door toward the parking lot. She was usually a very cautious driver but today she did break the speed limit a little. When she got to the

Carriage House she parked in the back, out of habit, and then realized it would've been quicker to go through the front. She ran in the back door, saying hi to the cooks as she breezed through the kitchen and through the swinging door to the floor of the restaurant.

Spotting her from the counter, Jerry motioned her over and presented her with the most gorgeous bouquet of flowers she'd ever seen. She sat them back down and fumbled for the envelope, ripping the card from it in a hurry. As she read it her smile broadened, 'I hope you're planning to call, I'm craving Huevos Rancheros. Mike.' She felt like a school child filled with excitement as she grabbed the flowers again and ran out the door, thanking Jerry and reminding him she'd be in Sunday morning. He waved, smiled and shook his head, wondering who'd just made her day.

When Amy walked into the school holding her flowers, the first person she saw was Elizabeth. Elizabeth looked like death warmed over and Amy didn't know what to say. She assumed things hadn't gone well and a quick summary from Elizabeth confirmed that. They walked as they talked and Amy glanced at her watch, realizing she had about twelve minutes left of her planning period. Elizabeth seemed oblivious to the flowers Amy was holding and as they entered her room and she sat them down, Elizabeth played with the petals of the flowers as she spoke. Amy didn't think she realized what she was doing but she listened to her friend as she spoke.

"And the worst thing is, he left the house last night and he isn't here today, he called in sick. I don't know where he is, what he's doing, if he's ok, God Aim what if he hurts himself? Oh my God I didn't even think about that until now, what if he tries to hurt himself?" and as she spoke she began crying. Amy didn't know what to do, time was limited, they both had kids to pick up in about 10 minutes and her friend was hurting. She hadn't had a chance to enjoy her flowers or call Mike but at this point her friend was more important.

"Listen Elizabeth, you need to pull yourself together. We have lunch coming up and we can talk then but for now, you need to be strong for your kids. Can you do that?" She had never seen Elizabeth like this. Elizabeth was always the strong one, always the one who didn't get flustered. Amy wasn't sure how to handle it and the only thing she could think of was to buy time until lunch. Elizabeth said she would do it and they'd meet at lunch in her room.

By the time they got to the gym there was no time left to call Mike and it looked like lunch wasn't going to work either. She was afraid he'd think she wasn't going to call but then he had no way of knowing if she'd even gotten the flowers yet. As much as it was killing her, he'd have to wait until after school for the call.

The lunch period was more of the same, tears, questions, wondering, guilt, none of which Amy knew what to do about. Lance's phone was turned off, all calls went straight to voice mail. Elizabeth didn't want to call his family and alarm them, they lived a few hours away but she didn't want to make that call. She'd only met them once, at the wedding and although they were nice, she wouldn't know what to say-'I don't want to give you grandkids?' That would go over well. She decided to wait and see how things went when she got home, he'd probably be there waiting to talk.

The rest of the day was long and drawn-out for both girls but for different reasons, one was excited, one was devastated. Amy felt a little hurt that she hadn't gotten to share her good news with her best friend but she chalked it up to the fact that Elizabeth's situation was much more serious.

Chapter Seven

"Friendship is the only cement that will ever hold the world together." – *Woodrow T. Wilson*

Amy's call to Mike occurred exactly one minute after her last student left for the day. She couldn't wait any longer. He answered after only two rings and sounded happy to hear from her. She thanked him for the flowers, they made small talk about his recent trip which he didn't seem to want to talk about, and then he asked her out to dinner that evening. For the next several weeks they were almost inseparable. They went out most evenings and were really enjoying getting to know each other. Mike had all the qualities Amy was looking for in a man. She had shared most of it with Elizabeth and from what she'd heard so far, Elizabeth approved of him as a suitable mate for her friend. Elizabeth, on the other hand, had not had a stellar few weeks.

On the same Friday afternoon that Amy made her call to Mike, Elizabeth went home to find all of

Lance's things gone. He had left a letter on the table and it took Elizabeth a few days before she could open it. She spent those days looking at the envelope, crying, reliving discussions, getting angry, talking with Amy and her mother, mostly her mother surprisingly, and wondering if she'd done the wrong thing. Both her mother and Amy assured her that everything she was feeling was normal and that she'd done the right thing by being honest with Lance, although her mother was heartbroken to know of the actual reason. She felt Elizabeth would be such a good mother but knew that regardless of her desire for more grandchildren, she'd have to accept her daughter's decision. Daniel's wife was due to deliver in a few months and that would keep her happy for a little while but she sure did like having grandbabies around.

When she did open the letter she was alone and it said pretty much what she thought it would. He was sorry, as much as she didn't want kids was just as much as he did want them, and there was no solution if neither would give. He said he'd file and pay for the divorce, she could have everything in the house and if she couldn't afford to pay the rent until the lease was up, he'd help out. The part that shocked her was toward the end of the letter. He told her he was going to give his notice at work and take accumulated leave days, meaning he would've met his contractual obligations but would not have had to return to work at all. He was going to move back to his home town, to his parents, until he got on his feet. He said it would be too difficult to see her every day. He apologized for putting her in the uncomfortable situation of having to answer everyone's questions but again, he said he just couldn't do it. She knew she was the stronger of them so his words didn't surprise her. He didn't leave any forwarding information and said his lawyer would handle everything and she should let the lawyer know if she needed anything. He said he still loved and cared for her and would help her if needed. He asked her to please give his best to her family and to extend his apologies to them as well and that was it. He didn't even sign his name, not that she didn't know who it was from but she figured everyone signed letters they wrote. She sat staring at the letter for the better part of an hour, not knowing what to do next, and when she finally got up from her chair she went back to her bed, laid down, and sobbed. Her marriage was over. Her lifetime was gone. She was all alone. And she didn't know what to do.

The rest of the school year was uneventful. In true Elizabeth style, she pulled herself together. She'd decided to go back to her maiden name, she'd had it a lot longer than she'd had Lance's name anyway. Those who knew her felt sorry for her, she had always been so strong and this had really knocked her for a loop but before long she was her normal self, occasionally she'd have a nostalgic moment and get a little sad. She'd heard from Lance's lawyer shortly after he left, the paperwork was in motion and there was nothing to fight over, anything they owned Lance allowed her to have. She was doing fine making ends meet with the rent and Amy was still paying the mortgage on the townhouse so that was covered. Her parents tried doting on her for a while but that quickly got old for Elizabeth and in true Elizabeth fashion, she let them know she was fine so they'd butt out. Amy and Mike had been dating since January and things were going very well for them, by all appearances it was serious. Mike had gotten word that he'd be going to Afghanistan in July for a year and while Amy was certainly not happy about it, she understood that it was his job and she respected him for what he did. June was quickly approaching and Elizabeth's lease on the house would be up, she would need to find a place to live. She thought about asking Amy to move out of the townhouse but she just couldn't do it, Amy was so happy being out of her parent's home and with school loans and a car loan, she really couldn't afford another place.

It was Memorial Day weekend and Amy finished her Sunday shift at the Carriage House, then hurried home to prepare for the get-together. This had continued after she moved in with Elizabeth's blessing, although Elizabeth rarely attended. But on Memorial Day weekend, Elizabeth showed up. Everyone was happy to see her, she'd been gone from the Carriage House for a year now and there were some new faces but also a few she recognized and it was good to see them and reminisce. Everyone knew not to bring up the subject of Lance but if they had, Amy felt sure Elizabeth would've handled it just fine. Elizabeth had met Mike months earlier and was very happy for her friend, he was a good man, and anyone could see that after spending just a few minutes with him. He'd been gone to California for a month of training, it was required for soldiers before they deployed, and Amy missed him terribly but school kept her busy. But now he was back and they were enjoying their last month together. Mike made himself very helpful at Amy's get-togethers, he helped cook, grill, clean up, and whatever was needed. He even played with Gina's kids when they attended with her, he thought they were cute.

On this particular day one of Gina's kids wasn't feeling well. Gina did the quick mom assessment and determined he was ok but suggested she'd probably better take him home and put him to bed. She'd been having a good time, something a single mom didn't get to do often, and Mike felt bad for her. From what he heard from Amy, her ex didn't ever spend time with the kids, a shame for them, but it also meant Gina didn't ever get a break. Without asking Amy, he offered the spare bedroom for Gina to have her son lie down. Gina glanced over at Amy who said, "Sure, I don't know why I didn't think of it, that room never gets used."

And just like that Amy and Mike both had the a-ha moment and they shared it with their facial expressions. It was the simplest solution ever and they couldn't believe they hadn't thought of it sooner. Elizabeth would move back to her own townhouse and share it with Amy. Perfect! Amy ran to Elizabeth to share the idea and Elizabeth smiled. She had thought of it earlier but wasn't sure it was best for their friendship. She had often heard that best friends should not live together. But the more she thought about it now, she remembered that she'd heard that about college roommates, she and Amy were grown women. Of course this could work. She'd do it. She'd move back in and share the townhouse with Amy. She wasn't crazy about taking the spare room but after all the moral support Amy had offered her the past few months, she didn't have the nerve to ask her to switch rooms.

School ended. Mike was preparing for his deployment and spending as much time with Amy as he could. She knew he'd get to come home for two weeks midway through his tour but a year was a long time and her feelings for him had grown strong. She had heard from other military-affiliated families that she needed to be strong to make it easier on him. After all, he was the one going into harm's way in less than desirable conditions. She planned to be very supportive while he was gone, sending him care packages and having her students write him letters, she thought he'd like that.

The day of departure snuck up on them before they knew it. She'd taken him to the area the soldiers were gathering at and the goodbye was tearful and difficult but Elizabeth was there for her when she walked into the townhouse. She hugged her friend hard while she cried in her arms. It took her a few days but she soon returned to her normal self and while she missed Mike already, she was looking forward to some summer fun with Elizabeth.

The girls didn't stay home much that summer. They took day trips to local historical sights and museums, weekend trips to the beach, a few lazy days at the local pool, a few trips to amusement parks, and shopping trips with, yes, their mothers! They often brought up their earlier thought that their moms were twins separated at birth, they were very much alike indeed. Daniel and his wife had added to Elizabeth's mother's collection of grandchildren and everyone was happy and healthy, the girls took some time to go to the hospital and visit when the baby was born. Amy looked upon the baby with wonderment and had lots of questions. She took pictures to send Mike, although he had never met Elizabeth's brothers she thought he'd enjoy seeing them. Elizabeth, as could be anticipated, smiled and said congrats, that was about it. Amy held the baby, Elizabeth said she'd wait until the baby was a little older.

Amy had decided to quit working at the Carriage House when school ended, now that the girls were splitting the rent she didn't need the extra cash as much. While it still could've helped her out, she decided to enjoy some time to herself that summer. She heard from Mike every once in a while, they tried to *Skype* occasionally, sometimes it worked but the connection wasn't always a good one. She faithfully mailed care packages to him containing his favorite snacks. The girls grew closer to each other that summer and for Elizabeth, every change in their friendship was something new, she'd never known anyone as well as she was getting to know Amy. They were going on two years of friendship and they sometimes wondered how they ever managed without each other in their lives.

The summer days zipped past them and before long the girls found themselves sitting at in-service again. They reminisced about the first in-service they'd attended together two years prior, when Elizabeth tripped over Amy's purse, and without thinking Amy blurted out that that's when they'd met Lance. As soon as she said it she apologized but Elizabeth assured her it was ok, she was over it. She couldn't give him what he wanted and he'd had a right to be happy, he did what he had to do and she didn't resent him for it. The divorce would be final in a few more weeks but it had been uneventful as far as divorces go. She hadn't talked to Lance at all, any communication went through their lawyers, he had wanted it that way and she was willing to oblige him that request.

October brought about both girls' birthdays and they celebrated together with a day off and indulged in mani/pedis, facials, massages, and a fancy lunch. They had a great time and toasted each other with champagne at their lunch. Toward the end of their meal Amy's phone rang. Elizabeth knew she wouldn't ignore it, it might be Mike and she wouldn't take the chance of missing his call. As soon as Amy looked at the screen, Elizabeth knew by her facial expression that it was indeed Mike. "Hi baby!" Amy said into the phone and excused herself to move to a quiet area to talk.

She was gone about 15 minutes. Elizabeth didn't mind, she spent the time checking and responding to emails on her phone. When Amy came back she shared that Mike would be coming home for his two weeks of R&R right around Christmas, the exact dates weren't known yet but that was the time frame and it would be perfect, Amy would be on break from school and they could spend the whole two weeks together. Mike didn't have any family, he was an only child, his parents had died when he was young and the grandparents who'd raised him had since passed on. Amy was really all he had, so of course he'd spend all of his time with her. She was all smiles as she shared the information with Elizabeth and deemed the news the best birthday gift ever. The girls smiled warmly at each other, they had become very close and both treasured their friendship. Things were going well in the townhouse, no issues or problems. Elizabeth had tried dating but said she just wasn't ready. She was over Lance but not sure she was ready for another heartache. Amy understood and supported her friend with her decision.

Chapter Eight

*"A friend is one that knows you as you are,
understands where you have been, accepts what you
have become, and still, gently allows you to grow."*
– William Shakespeare

The new school year was well underway. Elizabeth had been assigned a student teacher and this allowed her a little more free time during the school day. Amy was envious but the principal had asked Elizabeth to take on the task, not her. Maybe one day. On a warm October day, Elizabeth sauntered into Amy's room with a girlish grin on her face. Amy was in the middle of trying to explain subtraction with regrouping, a difficult concept for her second graders to grasp, but she couldn't miss the message that Elizabeth had something to share. She spent a few more minutes with her students and then assigned them some seat work, allowing her enough time to approach Elizabeth and see what was going on.

"Are you ready for this Amy?" she whispered. "The big boss just approached me about starting my master's program, and insinuated that I should get the degree in administration. He said I'm a natural leader and he thinks I'd be a great principal one day! Can you believe it? I never even considered it. What do you think? Be honest, you know I can't stand it when people sugar-coat stuff. Tell me the truth, would I be a good principal?" Amy looked at her friend quizzically. Misreading the look, Elizabeth blurted out, "You don't! You don't think I would be a good principal, I can tell by your face."

Amy took a step back and started shaking her head. "No, oh no, that's not it at all. I do think you'd be a good principal. What surprised me is that you even questioned it. You're so strong and confident, you have such good self-esteem, and you're a real go-getter. Of course you'd be an awesome principal. What an honor for him to approach you personally. How long would the degree take?" Secretly, again, Amy was a little jealous. She considered herself to be just as good a teacher as Elizabeth was, why didn't the principal approach her about this? But in true form, she provided the support, it was what best friends did. Not just a friend but Elizabeth's best friend. The smile returned to Elizabeth's face.

"Really Amy? Do you really think so? I know, you're right, I'm usually not one to doubt anything I want to do but this is such a big step. In charge of a school!" Amy walked toward her friend and embraced her in a hug. As she looked over Elizabeth's shoulder she saw her students staring at them.

"Ok you guys, back to work, Ms. Morrison just had a little something to share with me, that's all, you know you all chit-chat all the time, it was just our turn. Now back to work." And her students obeyed and got back to work as Elizabeth exited the room with a quick wave. Amy chastised herself a little for being jealous, Elizabeth deserved this, she'd had a rough year and this was a good thing for her. She should be proud and supportive, and that's just what she'd do as soon as the school day ended.

The bell rang and the children went through their dismissal routine. Amy loved her class this year. They were a great group of children with a lot of potential. When the last one was gone she reached for her purse to retrieve her cell. She was going to send Elizabeth some flowers to say congratulations. As she entered the number for information, she was suddenly startled by someone clearing their throat at the door. She looked up to see her principal standing there. "Hi Amy," he said, "Have a minute?"

She quickly tossed her cell back into her purse. "Sure, come on in! By the way, I love my group of kids this year. They're smart, polite, loving, and they show a lot of potential." Her principal smiled at her and motioned for her to sit down at the kidney-shaped table.

Pulling a chair up for himself, he said, "Amy there is a master's degree program at the college downtown I'd like you to consider. They have a specialization in administration and I think you'd be a fine principal one day. Of course it'll take a while and it's a lot of work, and once you get a principal's job, well, as you can see by my days, your time is no longer your own, you live at the school. But you're young and

108

single and just as you see a lot of potential in your students, I also see a lot in you. So I'd like you to consider it, and if there's anything I can answer for you or do to help you as you make your decision, I hope you'll speak up. I'm here to support you."

Amy just stared at him. She was flabbergasted. Never in a million years did she expect to hear what he just said. He had unknowingly put her at the same level as Elizabeth and to her that meant more than anything else he could've said to her. She sat pondering his words, not knowing what to say. She'd never thought of getting into administration, she wasn't sure she'd like it, she loved being with the kids and didn't know if she wanted to be in charge of a whole school. Sure it was nice to have his vote of confidence, but she always thought that if she got an advanced degree it would be in reading or something curricular. Searching for her words carefully, she replied, "Well thank you, I am certainly honored that you think I have the potential to do this, I'm just a little shocked and I'm not sure how to respond, I've never given this any thought whatsoever."

He smiled as he stood. "That's ok Amy, think about it. I'm surprised though, your BFF down the hall shouted 'yes' almost before I finished my speech to her. I'm sure she'll tell you about it later but I hope you'll consider it as well. Who knows, I only have a few years left before I retire, maybe one of the two of you could be running this school one day." For some reason Amy almost laughed out loud at that statement, but didn't, and thanked him again. She sat in wonderment after he left, feeling awfully pleased with herself, and forgetting all about the flowers for Elizabeth.

The girls met up at the townhouse later that evening. Elizabeth had gotten home first and was on her computer looking at the college criteria for the master's program. She wasn't one to let any grass grow under her feet, in fact, Amy wondered if she hadn't already enrolled in the program. Amy walked up behind her and read some of the content to herself. Three year program, scholarly writing expectations, administrative certification, all of these terms were things that were of no interest to her. She was honored to have been asked and she decided not to mention it to Elizabeth until she decided what to do about it but for now all she wanted to do was get out of her heels and relax. What she really wanted to do was talk to Mike but she knew that was at the mercy of the Army and the airwaves. She hated that they couldn't communicate daily but she accepted it and tried to make the most of the time they did get.

She went into her room, the master bedroom, and it dawned on her again, as it often did, that Elizabeth had never suggested they swap bedrooms. She kind of expected her to when she first moved back in but she hadn't and Amy was grateful, she loved the master bedroom with its own bathroom. She kicked her shoes off and into the closet and sunk down onto her bed. As she leaned back onto her pillow, she threw her arms above her head and closed her eyes. She imagined Mike being there, she loved him and missed him terribly and although he'd be home in another month and a half, she wanted him now. "Damn the Army," she said aloud without realizing it.

Elizabeth yelled back to her, "What did you say?"

Amy propped herself up on her elbows and yelled back, "Nothing. What are you doing for dinner?" Elizabeth came back to Amy's room and they talked about dinner. Then they talked about Elizabeth going to grad school. She was definitely going to do it and she'd start in January. Amy was happy for her and reaffirmed her decision not to mention the possibility of doing the same thing herself. She wanted this to be Elizabeth's thing and she was going to support her through it as best she could.

Elizabeth's mother had invited the girls over for Thanksgiving dinner and that meant Elizabeth's brothers and their families would be there too. Elizabeth wanted to go but had already said they'd make a quick exit after the festivities, she didn't like hanging around with 'all those kids' for too long. They were loud, they were messy, and they hung on her too much. Amy on the other hand loved the traditional family style day and happily interacted with the kids from time to time. Amy had received word that Mike would be home in about three weeks and she was ecstatic. Mike told her he wouldn't be giving her a date of return, he wanted to surprise her, he loved surprises, but she begged him not to keep the date a secret. She wanted to know when he was arriving so that she could get things ready and pick him up at the airport. He agreed but told her he didn't want to do anything special when he got home, he just wanted to relax and be with her, and Amy was fine with that. She spent the three weeks preparing for his visit.

Amy's parents had dropped a bombshell a few weeks earlier and told her they were moving to Germany, it was their country of ancestry and now that her father had retired, they were enjoying their time together and wanted to follow their dreams. They'd be leaving right after the first of the year so Amy and Mike would need to spend some of their time with them as well. Even though it was the right thing to do, Amy wanted to spend time with them, and she was sure Mike would too, but she really wanted as much time alone with him as she could get. He'd met her parents several times and they'd gotten along very well. Her mother had begun the inquisition the second time they were together, -Is this the one? Do you see yourself with him the rest of your life? Amy shooed her away and it was never brought up again although Amy really thought he might be her future husband. She reflected back on Elizabeth's brief marriage and frequently made mental notes to herself to cover all possible conflicts that could interfere with their happiness, knowing she couldn't possibly foresee them all but as far as kids went, she knew they both wanted them so that would never be an obstacle.

Amy's three weeks of planning went by quickly and soon the day arrived to go get Mike at the airport. She spent two hours deciding what to wear, trying on just about every outfit in her closet as well as a few of Elizabeth's and finally settled on one she

112

knew Mike would like. What she didn't know was that Mike could've cared less what she wore. He had plans of removing whatever it was as soon as they got back to her place but Amy was a girl and this is what girls did. When she was finally ready she walked into the living room and saw Elizabeth standing by the door with a suitcase. Amy stopped and stared. Surprised, she asked, "Where are you going?"

Elizabeth picked up the suitcase and nodded toward Amy's purse. "Grab your purse and let's go, my car's acting up so you're dropping me off at my mom's on your way to the airport. I don't want to be anywhere near your bedroom the next few nights so I'm staying over there but girl you owe me for this one," and she opened the front door with a smirk.

Tears sprang to Amy's eyes. Here was her friend giving up not just her bedroom but in reality, her own townhouse for her and Mike. The gesture meant so much to Amy and she ran to hug her friend. She thanked her over and over until Elizabeth convinced her that if they didn't leave now, she'd miss Mike coming off the plane. That did it and out the door they went. Elizabeth would be spending a week at her moms and that week included Christmas Eve and Christmas Day, she'd return to the townhouse the day after Christmas. That should give the lovebirds enough time to get reacquainted and she knew they'd be spending the time between Christmas and New Year's with Amy's parents, it was the least she could do for her friend who'd been so supportive of her throughout the past year.

The airport was filled with holiday travelers and Amy was grateful she was picking someone up and not trying to fight the lines to buy tickets, check bags, or get through security. She was told Mike would be arriving in his ACUs so she figured she should be able to find him easily, plus his height would help her find him. What she didn't anticipate was that he was coming in with about 80 other soldiers who would also be wearing ACUs. She was nearly in tears from happy anticipation already but when she saw the swarm of camouflage coming her way through the security gates, her tears poured out of anxiety…where was he? Was he in this group? Why couldn't she find him? Her eyes darted right and left, scanning the group of soldiers, she couldn't believe they were all so tall, how was she supposed to find Mike? Glancing around she began to wonder if there might be a second group of soldiers coming in from somewhere else when she felt his hand on her left shoulder.

As she turned a smile broke across her face and she choked back a sob before tears poured down her cheeks. She threw her arms around his neck and latched on to him, hugging him with all she had, pulling away every few seconds to kiss his lips while tears of happiness continued to run down her face. He hugged her back, whispering I love you into her ear and listening to her say it back. They'd shared their feelings before but this time seemed different, it meant something different to both of them, they had missed each other terribly and now they were together for two weeks. Two long weeks that would, undoubtedly, go by very quickly.

Mike pulled back while smiling and looked into Amy's eyes and asked if she was ok. She smiled and nodded and kissed him again. He kissed her back and then picked up his duffle bag. "Come on, let's get out of here. I have plans for you tonight," he said with a grin. Amy smiled as he wrapped his arm around her and escorted her out of the airport. Other airport patrons smiled at them, some clapped, some patted his back and thanked him for his service, but the only thing that mattered to him was that he had Amy in his arms once again.

Their homecoming night was unforgettable. He was thrilled to hear that Elizabeth wouldn't be there, not for any other reason than he didn't want to share Amy with anyone for a few days. He wanted her all to himself. The first night home he showered her with attention, kisses, passion, and lovemaking that went on throughout most of the night and it was better than ever. They whispered sweet nothings to each other throughout the night and other than that, there wasn't much talk, they only wanted to be with each other. Each day they slept in and then one of the two would cook breakfast. Some days they went back to bed for more reacquainting, other days they'd sit and talk or play cards and most nights they went out for dinner.

When Christmas Eve came they planned to attend a Church service with her parents. Neither was overly religious but they both had spiritual beliefs and had no objection whatsoever to attending the service.

When the candles were lit and the lights were lowered, the Church had a soft glow to it, It was beautiful and Amy's parents caught Mike and Amy gazing into each other's eyes more than once. They knew true love when they saw it and it's what they were seeing, they both believed their daughter had found the one. They invited the kids to their house for Christmas the next day and Amy spoke for both of them when she said they wanted to spend the morning together, then they'd come over for dinner.

On Christmas Day, the two exchanged the gifts they'd bought each other. Amy had given Mike a plaque depicting the Army emblem engraved with his name, unit, and rank as well as some cologne she knew he liked, a few shirts, and a keychain with a charm of his favorite football team. Mike had given her a beautiful necklace with her birthstone in it, matching earrings, some perfume, a *Coach* purse he'd seen her admiring back in June that he'd gone back to purchase before he left, and a sweater. She wondered when and how he did the shopping but guessed he'd done it before he'd left in July. They kissed and thanked each other and their kisses led them back to the bedroom. They couldn't get enough of each other and sheer happiness exuded from both of them. They had dozed off and were awakened by the shrill ring of Amy's cell phone.

It was Elizabeth calling to wish them a Merry Christmas. She spoke to Mike and welcomed him home, saying she'd see him later in the week, and then grilled Amy for details about the homecoming which

Amy dodged successfully. She knew Elizabeth would get the hint that she couldn't talk about it right now as Mike was sitting beside her but Elizabeth was dying to know if there'd been a ring involved in the activities of the last few days. She asked one more question, "OK Aim listen, I know you need to get off the phone but if you got an engagement ring, say, ok we'll see you tomorrow. If you didn't get one, say, we're off to my mom's, talk to you later." Amy laughed at her friends inquisitive mannerisms and ended the call with the second phrase. Elizabeth pouted a little, she had wanted her friend to get engaged, but then it dawned on her that Amy didn't sound the least bit disappointed when she responded with the latter of the two choices she had given her. She wondered for a split second if Amy was just saying she wasn't engaged, maybe she really was and wanted to surprise her, so she did what any good friend would do, she texted her the question. WERE YOU LYING? Within seconds the response came back. LOL! NO, MERRY CHRISTMAS! Elizabeth sighed, then threw the phone down on the dresser and headed out to help her mother prepare Christmas dinner.

Chapter Nine

"Friends have all things in common." -Plato

Amy and Mike had spent the rest of his R&R alternating between the bedroom and Amy's parent's house. They wanted to spend as much time with each other as they could but they both realized that once her parents moved, she wouldn't get to see them but once a year, if that, and that was only if her parents came home. Flights to Germany were expensive.

They spent New Year's Eve alone, in her bedroom. She couldn't believe that Mike had to leave in two days. Two days after that she'd be heading back to work. It wasn't fair, she told herself this all the time but at the same time she knew it was his job. He was up for a promotion in a few months and she was hoping he'd get it, he worked so hard. He'd made the Army his career and it meant a lot to him to be promoted through the ranks. She knew that if they did get married this would be her life forever so she'd might as well get used to it. He was set to come home for good sometime in June. Amy had asked him if there was a chance it'd be sooner but he said he doubted it.

The trip back to the airport was one of the longest she'd ever made and she cried the whole way there. Mike held her hand as she drove and tried to reassure her that the time would go quickly. In the back of her mind she remembered that she was supposed to be the strong one but she just couldn't, call her selfish but she wanted him there with her all the time. Their love had grown stronger with each passing day and without saying as much, they both knew in their hearts that they were headed for the alter one day, probably sooner rather than later.

As they approached the airport Amy initiated her turn signal to move into the lane leading to the parking area but Mike asked her to stay in the lane she was in. Confused, she did it, and realized they were headed to curb-side drop-off. "No Mike," she said when she realized what was happening. "I want to go in with you."

Mike sighed. "Amy if you go in there with me you're going to cry. Then I'm going to cry. And it's not going to be a pretty scene. Please, please, let me say good bye out here, please, do this for me. Please." She looked through the tears that had started forming again when he started talking. His face was pleading with her. It was then that she realized how much he really loved her. This was hard for him too. He hadn't shown it before but it was obvious now.

As the tears continued to fall she looked at him and said, "Is this really what you want?" He nodded, wiping at his eyes, and she knew he was on the verge of tears himself.

119

"Yeah baby, please, it is." She stared at him lovingly and then pulled her hand away from his and opened her car door. He sighed a heavy sigh of relief and did the same, then opened the backdoor and got his duffle bag out while she walked around to meet him. After shutting the back car door Mike dropped his duffle bag on the ground and grabbed Amy into an embrace. They hugged for a long time and Mike could feel the heaves of Amy's sobs on his chest as he held her in his arms. He pulled back and gazed into her eyes, wiping tears from them and said, "I love you baby, and I'll be back before you know it. Think of all the good times that are yet to come."

She smiled while the tears continued to roll down her face. "I know," she told him, "I know, and I'll be here waiting with open arms. You be safe and know that I love you with all my heart. I'll see you soon." One final kiss and he was gone.

She watched him walk through the sea of people and stifled her sobs until she got back into the car. As she drove away she thought about him, she missed him already, and from somewhere in the back of her mind she heard Elizabeth's voice. "Mike is your lifetime."

January was busy. School started back for the second semester, Amy's parents left for Germany, and Elizabeth started her college work. Amy had never told Elizabeth about their principal approaching her about the master's degree program. She had no intentions of pursuing it so why bother. It would've been great to carpool and study together but the classroom was where she wanted to be, not the office. More power to Elizabeth though, Amy supported her 100%.

Elizabeth started her classes on a Monday night in mid-January and came home to find Amy asleep on the couch. Thinking it highly unusual, she shook her slightly in an attempt to wake but not startle her. Amy's eyes opened and she glanced around, looking confused. "What time is it?" she asked as she raised herself up on her elbow.

Elizabeth pushed the hair out of her face. She felt sorry for Amy, knowing how much she missed Mike, and figured she'd probably been crying again and fell asleep. She'd been crying since he left it seemed. "It's a little after 9, Aim. How long have you been asleep?"

Amy looked around the room, as if the answer would come to her. "I have no idea," she said, "I honestly don't. I was just so tired and thought I'd lie down for a few minutes but it was light out when I did that, now it's dark." Elizabeth chuckled. She held out her hand and helped pull her friend to a sitting position.

"Come on," she said, "let's go do something. I'm wound up after that class. Wanna go grab something to eat or drink?" Amy really didn't want to but she knew Elizabeth well enough to know that she wasn't going to leave her alone until she said yes. The girls got ready and headed to Shorty's, it was early enough that smoking wouldn't be allowed yet, not till after 11 when the music started and they didn't plan to stay that long.

121

They found a booth in the corner and grabbed menus. They were known there and the waitress came running over to them as soon as she spotted them. "Take care of the regulars," her boss always said, and the girls knew that motto from their own time spent at the Carriage House. "What up girls?"

The waitress was punk, spiked hair and nose ring included, but she was really nice and a pretty good waitress. She knew Amy and Elizabeth had waitressed too, she could tell by their tips which were always generous. Amy wasn't really hungry but realized she hadn't eaten so she chose the spinach dip to avoid waking up hungry. Elizabeth ordered a turkey burger with fries and both girls ordered beers.

While they waited Elizabeth told Amy about her class, no hotties to speak of, the professor was fairly boring, and the workload would be heavy but she was up for the challenge and looking forward to fast-tracking the program. She had heard you could do the three-year program in two years if you piled on the classes and went in the summer as well. That had become her plan when she saw the kind of raise she'd get as a principal, she was ready. She no longer doubted her ability to do the job, in fact, she already saw some things at their school that she'd change if she was in charge. If anyone knew this it wouldn't surprise them, she was a take-charge kind of girl.

Their food arrived and Elizabeth devoured hers. Amy picked up a chip and dunked it into the creamy spinach dip. Elizabeth noticed and reached across to jab at her arm. "What's wrong Aim, you miss Mike?" Of course that's what it was, Elizabeth thought, or maybe she missed her parents? Nah, it was Mike, she was sure of it.

Amy twirled another chip in the bowl of dip and looked up at her, "I guess that's it, I don't know, I'm just so tired. Maybe we didn't get enough sleep over break and it's catching up with me. But hey I did hear from Mike earlier today, I almost forgot to tell you. And guess what? He's getting the promotion! They weren't supposed to announce it for a few more weeks but someone saw a list or something and word started getting around so they told him. He's going to be a Captain! I'm so proud of him." The smile on her face said it all, she was proud of the man she loved and Elizabeth was happy for her. And for Mike, he was a great guy and deserved to do well. She didn't know anything about his work habits in the Army but she could only imagine he did well. She kind of thought that she and Mike were alike in many regards, both eager and ambitious, both organized and dedicated to what they did, and both wanting to advance in their fields. She smiled back at her friend.

"That's awesome Aim, please tell him I said congrats," and she raised her beer glass to toast with Amy. It was then that she realized Amy hadn't touched her beer. "What's wrong? Why aren't you drinking your beer?" Amy looked at the beer in surprise herself, she didn't realize she hadn't taken a drink until just now. "I have no clue," she said as she raised the glass to meet Elizabeth's. They clinked the glasses. "To Mike" they said simultaneously.

The waitress appeared at the table just then and offered them their check, assuring them that if they wanted anything else she'd be right there to get it for them. They both reached for the check to see what their portion of it was but Elizabeth snatched it off the table first and said, "My treat. For Mike's promotion, kudos to both of you." Amy smiled and thanked her friend.

After paying the bill they headed home, passing some friends on the way out who begged them to stay but that wasn't their style, partying on a school night, and Elizabeth thought about the fact that she wouldn't be able to come into Shorty's anymore once she became a principal. She didn't care though, she was outgrowing the party scene and she wouldn't miss it at all.

Amy went straight to bed when she got home, could depression make you sleepy, Elizabeth wondered? Maybe it was good she didn't drink that beer, with alcohol being a depressant anyway. She hoped the next few months would fly by for Amy. She decided to go to bed herself, it was close to 11 PM and she had all her school work done. She had college homework but she had a week to get that done so she wasn't worried about it.

She felt like she'd just laid her head down when the annoying alarm clock went off. She'd gotten away from using the snooze button, she found that she was actually sleepier when she got up after using the snooze button. She didn't know if that had any merit to it but it was her thought and that made it reality. This was the time she despised not having the master bedroom, she had to go out into the hall to get to her bathroom. No more naked hall-walking, she had to wear her robe now, having Amy see her naked would just be too weird.

She showered and did her hair and make-up in the bathroom before heading back to her room to get dressed. Usually she'd hear Amy getting ready but this morning she heard nothing. It didn't really strike her as unusual until she finished dressing and went into the kitchen to make a bagel. Amy was at the kitchen table every morning well before Elizabeth came out of the bedroom dressed for work and this morning the lights were still out. Elizabeth knew Amy wasn't sitting in the dark and also knew she wouldn't have left that early without telling her. Something was wrong. She put her purse on the kitchen table and walked back toward Amy's room. The door was shut, which was normal, so she rapped lightly.

"Aim," she called quietly. She assumed Amy had overslept. Hearing nothing, she knocked a little louder, "Amy, you in there?" she called out. She heard a slight groan and then Amy's voice.

"Come in, I'm in the bathroom," was the reply. Elizabeth opened the door, the room was dark and she went in, taking a few steps before coming upon the bathroom door which was open. The light was on in the bathroom and Elizabeth immediately saw Amy sitting, arms curled around the toilet bowl with her head hanging down into it. She looked up at her friend and groaned again. "I've been in here puking for about an hour. It had to have been the spinach dip, that's the only thing I ate. God I feel awful. Do you think it's too late to call in for a sub?"

Elizabeth moved toward her friend, a little uneasy at first, she had no desire to see her heave into the toilet. "I think it is Aim, we're supposed to call in by 6 and it's 7:15, we have to be there in 15 minutes. What can I do to help?"

Amy groaned again and lowered her head back into the toilet bowl. Elizabeth anticipated the worst and took a step back but to her surprise Amy placed both hands on the bowl and pushed herself to first her knees and then her feet. She was moving in very slow motion and for each step she took toward Elizabeth, Elizabeth took a step back. "What do you need, let me help you," she offered. Amy flung her arm up toward the closet and mentally willed Elizabeth to get some clothing out for her. Elizabeth understood and did so.

Amy managed to get dressed while Elizabeth stood nearby in case she was needed. When she was finished she went back into the bathroom and brushed her teeth, then shooed Elizabeth out of the bathroom and then through the bedroom door as she followed her. "Do you mind driving me today?" she asked. Elizabeth shook her head and the girls headed out to the car, bags in hand. It was going to be a long day and she hoped she wouldn't get sick during class, there'd be no one to cover the kids if she had to run out of the room. She prayed she'd make it through the day and if she had time, she was going to call Shorty's and warn them that the spinach dip was bad.

Shortly after the school day started Amy began to feel better. Her kids sensed she wasn't at her best and behaved beautifully, working hard and completing all their work. By lunch she felt normal and ordered a school lunch since she hadn't had time to grab anything at home that morning. She still intended to call Shorty's and let them know she had gotten sick from their food but that could wait until after school, at the moment she was starving. Elizabeth had come in to check on her every chance she had that morning and was surprised to see her sitting with a plate of spaghetti in the faculty room. She joined her friend with her own plate and made small talk until it was time to go.

As they were leaving, their principal came in and made an announcement that he was looking for teachers to volunteer their time for a new curriculum committee. He explained that they'd meet one evening a week and would be responsible for reviewing and revising the elementary curriculum for the District and before he had finished speaking, Elizabeth's hand was up. A few others expressed interest before he left the room but none had done so as quickly as Elizabeth had. For a brief second Amy worried that her friend's plate would be too full with grad school and now this but she knew she'd find a way to make it work. Elizabeth was much more of a go-getter than Amy was and that was perfectly ok with Amy. Both girls assumed that Amy and Mike would probably marry within the next year or two and Amy was intent on settling in with babies right away, she was ready to start her family. True, they'd only been dating a year but when you knew, you knew, and Amy knew. It seemed everyone who knew them knew it too.

At the end of the day Elizabeth popped in to see if Amy was still feeling ok to which Amy replied, "Yeah, great, just still so darned tired. I think I'm going home to take a nap before I work on my lesson plans for tomorrow. If you get home and I'm not up by seven will you wake me?"

"Sure, but how are you getting home?" Elizabeth asked as she watched her friend, all packed up and heading toward the door. Amy stopped. Crap, that's right, her car wasn't there, she'd driven in with Elizabeth that morning. Elizabeth smiled and reached for her purse. "No sweat, take my car, I'll get a ride home with someone else." Wow, Elizabeth letting her drive the Camaro! She never let anyone drive her car and to be honest, Amy was a little nervous about it. Once she confirmed that Elizabeth was truly sure she was ok with it, Amy took the keys and headed home to nap.

Elizabeth did some work at school and then went to dinner with a colleague. This wasn't something she normally did and she was surprised at how enjoyable she found it. Denise was married but had no kids and neither she nor her husband wanted any. Elizabeth's mind drifted back to Lance but didn't dwell on it too long and she wondered if they'd discussed that *before* they decided to be married. She was really enjoying talking with Denise, they had more in common than she'd known and she was also thinking of going to grad school in the fall but in the field of curriculum and instruction. They both had dessert after dinner then paid their bills before Denise drove Elizabeth to the townhouse. On the way there

Elizabeth shared the news of Mike's promotion, their friends at school had not met Mike but had heard all about him and they were happy for Amy. She told Denise that she suspected they'd be married with kids before too long and she was happy for them. Denise dropped her off around eight, she'd long forgotten about Amy's wake-up call.

She remembered as she walked in the front door. Oh well, so Amy got an extra hour of sleep, no big deal.

She walked back toward Amy's room and pushed the door open, calling Amy by name. Amy jumped up with a start as Elizabeth apologized for being an hour late and Amy just looked at her as if she didn't know what she was talking about. Elizabeth tried to reiterate the story but Amy waved her arm at her, indicating she just wanted her to leave her alone. "I'm going back to sleep, see you in the morning." Elizabeth asked her if she needed anything and then backed out of the room and shut the door. She hoped Amy wasn't coming down with something, not only would that make her friend sick it would also put her in jeopardy of getting sick and she had no time for that. Elizabeth went about her usual routine the rest of the night and headed to bed herself just a few hours later.

The following morning was almost like déjà vu for Elizabeth, from the alarm to the shower to getting dressed to walking into the dark kitchen. No Amy. Instinctively she headed back toward Amy's room and saw that the door was shut. There was no light protruding from underneath the door so she knocked lightly and then entered on her own. She saw the glow of the bathroom light from beneath the closed bathroom door. Oh no, Amy was sick again. What could it be this time? She hadn't eaten anything that Elizabeth was aware of yesterday other than the school lunch and if it had been bad, Elizabeth would've been sick as well.   She tapped on the bathroom door. "Aim, again?" She heard the familiar groan and entered without waiting for the invite. "Girl what is going on with you?" Elizabeth asked. "This is two days in a row and it can't be the food you ate, do you think you have a stomach virus?" Amy slowly lifted her head up to face her friend. Stomach virus? Doubtful, she thought. The girls stared at each other for a few seconds and suddenly it was as if Elizabeth read Amy's mind. She inhaled sharply and raised her hands to her mouth, staring at Amy the whole time, unable to move. Searching for the right words, she couldn't find them so what came out was, "You're not!"

Tears streamed down Amy's face but Elizabeth couldn't move. She still couldn't think of the right words to say so she said, "You're not Amy, tell me you aren't pregnant!" Amy pushed herself to her feet, instinctively holding her belly, and moved toward Elizabeth who still stood paralyzed.

"I don't know, I don't know, do you think I am? I'm afraid I might be Elizabeth, I don't know what else could be wrong with me, and worse than that I don't know what to do. I'm scared, I'm so scared, and what if I am? What do I tell Mike? What do I tell my parents? How could I let this happen?" Each question came out with a higher pitch and level of urgency than the previous one and Elizabeth knew she had to pull herself together and be there for her friend. As quickly as she had frozen in time when the realization hit her, she just as quickly rushed toward Amy and hugged her hard while Amy sobbed into her neck. Elizabeth stroked the back of her friend's head and let her cry for a while. For a split second she recalled a similar situation in which the roles had been reversed. Elizabeth's situation had ended well, Amy's would too. She pulled back and looked her in the eye.

"Amy, look at me, look at me, you need to hear me." Amy raised her head and looked Elizabeth in the eye, still crying but ready to listen. "OK, first of all, I think we both know how this could've happened and it isn't all your fault, I am willing to bet Mike was there too. And if you are, if, and we don't know that you are but if you are, it's going to be ok. If you are, you're going to become a mommy, and you're going to be an awesome one. If you are, you're going to tell Mike he's going to be a daddy, and he'll be a great one. And if you are, you're going to tell your parents they're going to be grandparents, and they will be thrilled! It's not like you're a teenager with no job who doesn't have a steady boyfriend. You have everything you need in place to have a happy ending if you are pregnant and that's a big if. The first thing we have to do is get you a pregnancy test and find out. Now, are you able to get yourself dressed because once again, it's too late to call for a sub and we have to go to school? I'll drive and we can swing by the drug store and grab a pregnancy test on the way but you're going to have to hurry. Can you do it?"

Elizabeth's words sank into Amy's head and she didn't remember doing it but she apparently nodded her head. Elizabeth went out to get their things together. Amy got ready quickly and the next thing she knew she was in her classroom with a small Bailey's Drug Store bag in her purse. Her planning period was at 10 and that's when she'd take the test. Elizabeth said she'd be there with her. They contemplated taking the test at the end of the day but Amy knew she couldn't wait that long and Elizabeth didn't think she could either.

Just like the previous day, Amy felt better shortly after the day started and for a fleeting minute she thought it was just a fluke, that she'd just had a two-day bug, but deep-down she was pretty sure that wasn't it. Amy checked the classroom clock nearly every minute and time was just dragging. She thought about calling for someone to cover her class so she could go to the bathroom and take the test but then she wouldn't have Elizabeth with her. So she waited and when Elizabeth entered her room at 10:01 she grabbed her purse which contained the bag that held her future and ran toward the faculty bathroom. The girls went in together and locked the door.

Denise had been running copies in the faculty room and saw them go in, she looked strangely toward the door but didn't think too much of it, she knew they were good friends. Inside the girls went through the motions and Amy stayed seated the entire time. After five of the longest minutes either one had ever endured, Elizabeth reached down and handed the stick to Amy and then grasped Amy's empty hand with her own. Maintaining eye contact and speaking to each other silently, her eyes slowly began to wander downward toward the stick. When Amy's eyes finally reached the target, Elizabeth didn't need to see it, she could tell by the look on Amy's face. Amy burst into tears immediately and hung her head in shame.

Elizabeth moved toward her and hugged her, it was all she could do, and she repeatedly said, "It's going to be ok, it's going to be ok."

Amy stood back and wiped at her red eyes. "Oh my God, I don't even know what to do first. Elizabeth what do I do? Tell me what to do. I can't just call Mike but I feel like he should be the first to know. I don't want to call my parents just yet. Should I go tell the boss? Tell me what to do." Elizabeth could see how anxious and nervous she was. It dawned on her that for most women, this was the happiest moment of their lives but here was her friend, devastated, and she didn't know what to do. "OK, first we're going to make a doctor appointment, we want to make sure, these things can give false positives," she said nodding toward the stick.

"No Elizabeth, it is what it is, I will make a doctor appointment but let's face it, I'm pregnant," and with that came more tears. Elizabeth had to think quickly and this was the furthest thing from her comfort zone. She informed Amy that they were going to clean her face up and go back to teaching and try to pretend nothing was different. They'd figure it out at home tonight.

And that's what they did. It wasn't easy, every time Elizabeth thought she had Amy ready to go back to class, she'd burst into tears again. By now Denise had left the faculty room so they didn't need to make any excuses to her which was a relief and they finally headed down the hall to their classrooms. It was going to be a long day for sure and most likely, a longer night at home.

Chapter Ten

"Friendship is the golden thread that ties the heart of all the world." - John Evelyn

The first thing they did when they got home that evening was "google" obstetricians in the area. She wanted to make an appointment to confirm what she already knew and find out what she needed to know and do in order to assure a healthy pregnancy. After reading recommendations on each, she settled on Dr. Beachy. Elizabeth thought it was very appropriate that his name had 'beach' in it since they both loved the beach so much, she said it was an omen and Amy laughed for the first time in a while.

Sitting at the dinette table, they talked about everything imaginable and unimaginable that night. Amy had so many questions and Elizabeth was of no help whatsoever. However, she was able to get her friend to laugh a little more but the underlying seriousness of the situation still remained clear in their minds. Amy was adamant that she wasn't going to tell anyone until she talked to Mike and reiterated that about a hundred times during their conversation. Elizabeth stood and offered to get drinks for them. Amy asked for a soda and then thought about the baby and changed her mind to milk. Elizabeth pointed out that she was already making 'good mom' decisions and they both laughed.

"I guess it won't be about me anymore, or what I want," Amy joked.

As she was pouring the milk, Elizabeth heard the distinctive ring of Amy's cell. It was coming from the counter near the fridge. She sat the milk down and picked the phone up, glancing at the screen. Turning her eyes toward Amy, she grinned and said, "Looks like you won't have to wait long to talk to Mike," and she handed Amy the phone and retreated to her own bedroom with her soda.

The conversation went well, better than Amy expected it to. Part of her thought Mike would be angry but he wasn't. A very small part of her thought he'd break up with her, feeling as if she'd trapped him but he didn't. They both wondered aloud how it could've happened because they used protection but when Mike mentioned it he wasn't accusatory and he had no doubts about Amy's faithfulness. She didn't have an answer as to how it happened any more than he did but they both knew condoms weren't 100% effective in preventing pregnancy. In the end he said he loved her and they'd get married as soon as he got back and they'd start their family, he said he felt that's where they were headed anyway, this just expedited things a little. He said he wished they could've gone the traditional route where he'd ask her parents for her hand, propose and put a ring on her finger and get married first but he kind of shrugged it off and said that most of his life had not been traditional so why should this be any different? He chuckled as he said it, probably in hopes of making her laugh a little, and it worked. He joked that his news paled in comparison to hers but shared that his promotion would be happening in theater, meaning while he was deployed and they'd have two reasons to celebrate when he got home. They talked about their next steps. He wanted Amy to tell her parents as soon as she was ready and said if she'd take her laptop along to her doctor appointments he'd try really hard to *Skype* with her. She knew there was no guarantee but was thankful he was showing so much interest so early on. He truly was a great guy and she felt very fortunate to have him as the love of her life and the father of her baby. They ended the call with sentiments of love and Amy felt much better than she had before the call.

She went back to Elizabeth's room and lay across her waterbed, sharing all the details of the call with her. Elizabeth smiled and although she wouldn't admit it, she felt a little envious of the love Mike was displaying. Elizabeth missed being loved but knew it would happen again for her when the time was right. She reminded Amy that Mike was her lifetime although she didn't buy into the categorizations the way Elizabeth did. She continued to tell Amy that she must just be a season to her since she'd be moving out to live with Mike when he got home. They both laughed at that and Elizabeth told her that as much as she'd loved having her there and as much as she'd miss her, she had to be honest and admit that she would be glad to have her place back to herself again. With grad school and the curriculum committee she was serving on, her schedule was getting fuller and fuller and she sometimes felt guilty that she didn't do her fair share of cleaning and upkeep at the townhouse. Amy had never complained though, she'd been an awesome roommate and Elizabeth was truly going to miss her.

February, March, and April went by quickly. Elizabeth got busier with all of her commitments and even took on another one, she was a Teacher's Assistant, referred to as a TA, for her professor in another one of his classes which took her to the college on Wednesday nights as well as on Mondays for her own class. Amy had been to her doctor four times and she really liked him, he was very comforting and caring and she felt as if she and the baby were in good hands. Mike had successfully *Skyped* with her for one of the appointments but it was a fairly uneventful one, they weighed her, felt around her belly a little, and told her they'd see her next month. They estimated her due date as September 17th which was fine, Mike would be home and other than the health of the baby, that was all that mattered to her. It would be the start of the school year but she'd be taking a maternity leave. Mike had mentioned her not working at all while the baby was little but they hadn't really made any decisions. They discussed when they wanted to get married, Mike wanted to go to the court house and take care of it as soon as he got back in June but Amy refused, they might not be doing things the traditional way but she was going to have a traditional wedding and she couldn't do that when she was seven months pregnant. She was fine waiting until after the baby was born, once she'd lost the baby weight and could fit into her normal size clothing. He reminded her that if they were married the Army would pay her medical bills but she reminded him that she had great insurance of her own through work and she didn't want to get married to suit the Army. He didn't argue, he just wished he could make her his wife sooner rather than later.

She'd finally called and told her parents the news in March. She was anticipating anger and was shocked when she heard them shriek with exhilaration. She was their only child and their only hopes of grandchildren were with her. They couldn't have been happier for their daughter and her boyfriend and looked forward to welcoming him into their family. They wanted to be kept abreast of all doctor appointments and updates and if there were sonogram pictures, they wanted to see them. They asked her when she wanted them to fly home and she said she'd get back to them. She was happy that they were happy and everything seemed to be falling into place.

Amy started showing in early May, about four months into her pregnancy. While the doctor had estimated her exact date of conception, she wasn't so sure considering all the love-making they'd done while Mike was home on R&R, it literally could've been just about any day in the two week period. She needed to go shopping for maternity clothes and asked Elizabeth

139

to go with her, half expecting her to decline, Elizabeth had been so busy lately and was clearly on a career path. She had told Amy a few weeks ago that she thought she would be one of those women who are married to their career, she didn't want or need a man and everyone knew she didn't want kids, that hadn't changed. Amy joked that Elizabeth's maternal clock had dead batteries.

But Elizabeth did agree to go and Amy was glad, with her mother in Germany and Mike in Afghanistan she really didn't have anyone else. They spent an entire Saturday going mall to mall and looking for anything maternity. Elizabeth would shake her head in disgust at the clothing Amy tried on, not in front of Amy, she couldn't help that she needed it, but the thought of needing it was what got to her, why would women do this to their bodies? She just didn't get it. Now if you could have the kid without gaining weight, getting sick…nah, even then she wouldn't want to have children but if she had to, that would be the way she'd want to do it.

As they shopped they passed lots of families and Amy smiled in anticipation of being one of them soon. Elizabeth had asked her how many kids she thought they'd have and she said they'd never really discussed it before but for sure more than one. She asked her if they wanted this one to be a boy or a girl and concluded with "and don't say 'as long as it's healthy' – everyone has a preference." Amy had to think for a moment, of course she'd thought about it but she really hadn't come to a conclusion. Mike hadn't expressed his preference yet, they got to talk so

140

seldom and when they did it was the usual catch-up stuff and while that included talk about their unborn baby, they'd never gotten around to discussing the gender. She wondered if they'd want to find out before the baby was born, her doctor had told her they would probably be able to tell during May's appointment. She made a mental note to ask Mike the next time they talked.

When the girls finally stopped for lunch, Amy was famished. She was trying to watch her food intake to avoid gaining too much weight but at the same time she needed to eat regularly. The benefit of the food court was that they could each get what they wanted. Elizabeth opted for Chinese while Amy got a grilled chicken salad. They sat and talked for what seemed like hours. Satisfied with the clothing purchases she'd made, Amy said she was ready to head home. Elizabeth agreed, citing lots of work to get done, and they left the mall smiling.

School ended June 10th, Mike came home June 11th, and Amy had a doctor appointment on the 12th. Everything was happening at once but she was handling it well and was happier than ever. She'd found an apartment in town for her and Mike. Because they weren't married they couldn't get housing on post but that was ok with her, she was pleased with what she'd found and it was in their price range. She had moved her things in on June 1st with the help of several colleagues from school (they wouldn't let her lift anything). They'd been very supportive of her when she made the announcement that she was expecting, they were excited. Her principal helped her work through the HR process to take leave and assured her he'd hold her job as long as she wanted him to, she was a terrific teacher and he didn't want to lose her. They decided not to find out the gender of the baby until Mike was home and that day had come.

They sat in Dr. Beachy's waiting office holding hands and looking at a Parents magazine. Amy was reviewing an article on baby proofing your home. Mike was looking over her shoulder, reading about every other word and understanding very little of it when the nurse called them back. Once in the tiny exam room the nurse took Amy's vitals and weighed her, still within the normal range and she was glad to hear it. She left the room and returned almost immediately with a big machine on wheels that Mike had never seen before. The nurse began preparing things on a tray and one of the things Mike saw was a wand. Not knowing what it was for, he picked it up to get a closer look. The nurse pulled it from his hand and laid it back down as she shot a grin toward Amy. "These items are sterilized for use sir, I'm sorry but you can't handle them." Amy giggled, mostly because she knew Mike had no idea what he'd just picked up and she wasn't going to tell him. He'd see soon enough.

The nurse left and told them the doctor would be in. Mike found himself a little nervous, this was all new to him. He looked around the room, taking it all in, and then reached over and took Amy's hand. He raised it to his lips and kissed it before asking her, "Do you have any idea how much I love you?"

She smiled and nodded her head. "I do, and do you know how much I love you, Captain?" He leaned up to where she was sitting on the exam table and kissed her lips gently. Never had he felt so strongly about another human being in his life, and he wondered how he'd feel about the baby when it was born, would he love it immediately? If not how long would it take, after all he didn't fall in love with Amy the second he saw her, although he had to admit he was quite smitten. "So," Amy began, "are we going to find out if it's a boy or a girl?" She wanted to but was willing to wait if he wanted to. He pursed his lips and rubbed his chin.

"Hmm. Well, I suppose if we find out we can prepare a little better with decorations, clothes, and a name. On the other hand, it might be nice to be surprised in the delivery room. What do you think?"

Amy considered his words, and then replied, "I think I'll let it up to you. I'm ok either way. You decide." Mike smiled and nodded just as the doctor walked in.

Mike stood. The men made quick introductions and the doctor thanked Mike for his service to their country. Mike nodded and sat back down. The doctor began reviewing Amy's chart. Now, let's see how we're doing here, Miss Amy. How have you been feeling? Any problems?" he asked as he looked over her chart. Amy answered his questions, all had been fine and she felt great. He expressed his approval of her weight gain thus far and encouraged her to keep it up. Then he picked up the wand and said, "Now lay back and let's take a look at this movie star on the big screen, what do you say mom and dad?" Mike glanced at Amy curiously, then back at the wand, then back at Amy. She grinned as the redness began rising in Mike's cheeks.

Amy squeezed Mike's hand then and lay back as the doctor had asked her to do. As the doctor moved the wand below the sheet, Mike kept his eyes glued to the computer-like screen. He had no idea what he was looking at but he was fascinated. Amy watched too, but she didn't seem as enthralled as Mike was which made sense as she'd been through this several times before. The doctor moved the wand some more and Amy flinched a little, Mike looked startled but Amy shook her head, no I'm fine, she was letting him know. The image on the screen moved and bounced all over the place, surely the baby wasn't moving like that, no, he realized, the wand was moving around the baby. Mike was overwhelmed, he had no idea there was so much involved in a doctor's visit.

The doctor spoke then, "So did we decide if we want to know the gender or not?" Mike looked at Amy and she shrugged and smiled, leaving the decision to him.

"You mean you can tell from that?" Mike asked, pointing toward the screen with a surprised look on his face. Amy chuckled again, she was enjoying watching his reactions. The doctor reassured him that yes, he could tell, the only thing that remained unknown was whether he was keeping it a secret or not. Mike took a deep breath, squeezed Amy's hand again, and nodded at the doctor.

Dr. Beachy turned the monitor completely toward the couple so they were staring the baby in the, well, whatever part of the baby that was, and smiled at both of them before announcing, "Say hello to your son."

Elizabeth had decided to take two classes that summer. Along with her TA position at the college, she barely had a moment to herself and felt badly that she couldn't help Amy move out but she made up for it by going over and unpacking everything for her. She wouldn't let Amy help at all and she ended up putting things in places Amy would later move them from but she was helping from the heart and Amy appreciated it. Amy had wanted everything to be perfect for Mike when he got home. The apartment was set up other than the baby room. Amy was waiting for him to come home to do that with her. They'd talked about it and agreed. He wanted to be a part of everything since he'd missed the first five months of the pregnancy.

Elizabeth stayed busy throughout June and July and early August. She had had very little time to check in or spend time with Amy but she knew Mike was there so she felt reassured that all was well with her friend. As she knew she would, she missed having Amy at the townhouse but enjoyed having her freedom back, and her master bedroom.

The hot days of August had begun and in-service was set for the fourth week of the month. Sometime during the second week of August Elizabeth was working in the college library finishing up some work for one of her classes. She was engrossed in her work and was somewhat startled when her cell phone vibrated against the bare tabletop, alerting everyone around her that she had violated the no cell phone rule for the library. She glanced around quickly and saw that those in her immediate range had heard the annoying noise and did indeed appear to be annoyed based on the looks on their faces, but she didn't notice any of the librarians nearby and she sighed a sigh of relief. She had seen them ask people to leave for cell phone use, they took that rule seriously.

She picked up the phone then and glanced at the screen. She saw her school's name displayed on the screen as the phone continued to vibrate in her hand. She stood and hustled toward the door, depressing the 'answer' button before she got outside simply to keep it from going to voice mail. Surely the caller would hear the background noise and not hang up. Once she was safely outside the library doors, she put the phone to her ear and said hello.

It was her principal and he was calling to inform her that the School Board had approved each elementary school to have an administrative intern for the coming year. For years principals had begged to have assistant principals, the managerial work load was simply too much for principals to handle if they were expected to focus on instructional leadership, but the Board stood solid that it was too cost prohibitive. This coming year, however, they'd worked with the local college and created a working intern position. The position was for one year only and would allow administrative candidates already enrolled in their program to work full-time as an administrative intern in one of the district schools, with full pay. This would reduce the costs to the Board to only those of a replacement teacher for a year, much cheaper than paying another administrator. A win-win for everyone involved.

Elizabeth's principal finished explaining the opportunity and expressed his interest in having her as his intern. He wanted to know if she'd be interested. Elizabeth thought about it for almost two seconds before she said yes, of course she was interested. What an opportunity for her! She asked for the details of how to apply and he directed her to the human resources department but shared that each principal was given full discretion to select who they wanted for the position so she wouldn't need to apply or interview, it was just a matter of paperwork. She hung up with a huge smile on her face, everything was going her way and she couldn't be happier.

She turned to re-enter the library and once inside, she saw a very good looking guy staring at her from across the lobby. She was still smiling and he must've assumed she was smiling at him, so he smiled back and gave her a little wave. Oh my gosh, she thought, he's flirting with me. As she walked toward the library entrance he started walking toward her. He stopped her short of the door and introduced himself as Josh. He shared that he was a grad student working on an advanced business degree and she followed by sharing her information. He was very good looking and had a deep sexy voice that had her lingering on his every word. After a little more small talk he asked if she'd like to have lunch as it was nearing the noon hour and she said yes. She gathered her things from the library and off they went to a local café.

Amy walked into the District's HR department late that afternoon to fill out her maternity leave paperwork. They had decided she would not work from the beginning of the school year since she was due so shortly after it started and Mike was thrilled with her decision. She'd let a sub start off with the class from day one, that would be easier on the kids than having her for a few short weeks and then transitioning to a sub. Sure, that meant she'd have a lot more work to do when she got back to get them where she wanted them and if it were up to Mike, she wouldn't be going back. She was still thinking about that option. She did love her job but she loved her own son even more and the thought of being with him for all of the important moments was appealing. Money-wise she didn't have to work but she absolutely had to stay employed at least until they were married for insurance purposes.

As she walked the hall toward the office she was directed toward, she turned a corner and nearly ran right into Elizabeth. Both girls were a little shocked and grinned at each other before hugging. They exchanged quick greetings and then Elizabeth asked as she patted Amy's round belly, "How's little man doing?" She had known since the day Amy knew that it was a boy and she was happy for them. She had yet to go back over to the apartment though, there was just no time. She could see Mike with a boy, he would do

148

all the right dad things with him, and truth be told if she had ever wanted kids she'd have wanted a boy, she didn't feel like she would ever bond with a girl the way moms and daughters are supposed to.

Amy shared that the baby was fine but that she and Mike were having a disagreement. Just like Elizabeth, Mike was on the fast career track and he was being pressured to apply to attend a year-long school in Kansas. Not only would attending this advance his current career opportunities but it would move him toward another promotion much quicker if he did so. The class started in January and he wanted them to have the baby, get married, and relocate to Kansas for the year. Amy was very proud of him and wanted him to advance but she simply didn't want the Army dictating their moves and decisions. Mike reminded her often that he didn't necessarily have that choice, the Army did indeed dictate what he'd be doing, at least if he wanted to do well, and she was always quick to remind him that they didn't own her. Yet.

Elizabeth listened and sympathized and then shared her own news of the administrative internship, thus her presence at HR. Amy was ecstatic for her, she knew Elizabeth wanted to climb the career ladder and thought about how about similar her friend and Mike actually were. The difference was that in Mike's world (that being the man world) he could have the career and the family while in Elizabeth's world (that being the female world), she was expected to choose. It didn't seem fair but it was what it was.

The girls said their goodbyes and went about their ways with the promise of having lunch together soon. They had barely seen each other all summer, Amy busy with Mike and the baby and Elizabeth busy with school. They'd missed each other and needed to get caught up. Elizabeth made it a point to make a lunch date with Amy for the following week. Once in-service and school started she'd have no time whatsoever so she wanted to make sure and get it scheduled now. She had a feeling she was in for the ride of her life this year.

True to her word, Elizabeth made arrangements with Amy for lunch the following week. She had already started her internship and was up to her ears in work preparing for in-service week but she forced herself to take time for lunch with Amy. They'd found a sub for her, a young girl just out of college who, had she met the girls back when the two of them had first met, probably would've been one of them. Upon hearing this Amy felt a little better about not starting the year with her kids. It wasn't an easy decision but she honestly felt it was best for the kids and she'd gotten so pregnant that occasionally her ankles swelled beyond belief. Both sitting and standing for long periods of time were part of her job so having the sub from the start was probably best for her as well.

During lunch the girls chatted endlessly, they both had much to share having not been together most of the summer. Amy spoke mostly of baby things, especially about how she was decorating the baby's room, it was going to be a jungle theme, but also shared that her parents were doing well in Germany and enjoying life. They regularly told her how excited they were for the arrival of the baby and expressed their happiness that they were the grandparents and not the parents. They could spoil him, have fun with him, tire him out and leave. Elizabeth asked if they'd *Skyped* but Amy just laughed, reminding her of their lack of technology skills. She'd shared their comments about the baby with Mike and he found himself feeling a little sad that he had no grandparents to offer their child. Amy assured him that even though they were in another country, they'd spoil him enough for both sets of grandparents. They'd decided to name the baby Johnathan Michael, Johnathan after Mike's dad and Michael of course, after Mike.

Elizabeth asked about the disagreement they'd been having last week about Kansas and Amy responded, "Oh it gets better, now he says that after the year in Kansas , he can get an assignment in Germany for three years but he can't get that assignment unless he does the schooling in Kansas. We would be near my parents. He tossed that in as a bonus I guess, to get me to agree. I haven't told him yet but I am leaning more toward the idea, I mean, my parents would love to be near their grandchild but they made it clear they're not moving back to the states. This would be a good thing for them, and I could always teach overseas in a military-based school. Of course I'd go to Kansas with him, if he gets in, there's nothing keeping me here, but in order for the Army to allow me to go with him we'd have to be married." She smiled as she finished, she knew she'd all but resigned herself to the fact that they were going. "I haven't told him yet but I probably will tonight. It'll make him happy. So get ready for a wedding sometime in November or December, I need a maid of honor."

Elizabeth shrieked with happiness and was secretly happy that she knew Amy's decision before anyone, even Mike. After Amy's news was shared Elizabeth started. "Well," she said, "I've been seeing this guy named Josh for a few weeks. It's not serious and it probably won't get serious, he's good looking, nice, fun, but Aim I want to focus on my career now, I don't want to get tied up in a relationship and set myself up for another heartbreak. I want to live for me, no one else, just me. I know that's selfish but I can't help it, that's how I feel. I'm just being honest."

Amy smiled and reached over to touch Elizabeth's hand. She loved her friend; she knew the huge heart that most others didn't. She needed to reassure her friend. "There's nothing wrong with that Elizabeth. Maybe one day you'll feel differently but for now, you have to follow your dreams. Do what makes you happy. If you're involved with someone then you have to focus on his happiness too and while there's nothing wrong with that either, it's just not for you right now. Focus on you, become the Superintendent if you want to, but make your choices for *you*. To quote you and your mom, your job is your lifetime right now, she smirked."

Elizabeth smiled at her friend's cynicism but then looked at her with compassion. Amy was really the only one she had ever gotten close to, the only one she shared secrets with, the only one whose opinion of her mattered. Her best friend. As far as she was concerned Amy was her lifetime. But now her best friend would be leaving and Elizabeth was not clueless to the fact that she'd need to start separating from her to avoid a huge heartbreak and loss when the time came for her to leave. Sure, she'd be her maid of honor and do all the things that come with the role but she'd have to get ready to say goodbye to this season of her life.

Overall lunch had been like a school-girl reunion, a good one, and both girls enjoyed the time together. They stayed at the restaurant for an hour and a half and found they didn't want to part ways when Elizabeth finally said she had to get back to school. They hugged tightly and told each other to stay in touch, which they knew they would. Elizabeth hurried out the door after paying the whole check and Amy watched her as she hustled toward her car. Such a go-getter, such an ambitious, self-motivated, energetic person Elizabeth was, and for a brief, fleeting moment, Amy found herself a little envious.

Chapter Eleven

"Friendship improves happiness, and abates misery,
by doubling our joys, and dividing our grief."
                    – Marcus Tullius

The summer heat had made the pregnancy somewhat
uncomfortable for Amy but she knew she wasn't the
only one that had ever happened to. She dealt with it as
best she could but she surely welcomed the cooler days
September brought with it. She'd told Mike of her
decision to marry him. She told him to apply for the
schooling in Kansas and said she'd go with him, then
on to Germany, and both Mike and her parents were
thrilled.

        Pete and Lois were set to arrive in the states in
about three more weeks. They couldn't wait until the
last minute to get airfare or the price would've been
too high so they planned to arrive right after her due
date. Amy's mom knew that most babies made their
debut late and was hoping her grandchild was not the
exception. She purchased their tickets with confidence
and took comfort in knowing they'd be there. The
only question was whether the baby would welcome
them or they'd welcome the baby.

Amy spent the days nesting, adding final touches to the baby's room, cleaning around the house as well as she could (she couldn't lift or move anything heavy), and she cooked dinner for Mike each night. She loved cooking for him and had recently been delving into cookbooks to find unique and exotic recipes for him. She chuckled when she thought of the old saying, 'The way to a man's heart is through his stomach.' She'd never really cooked for Mike when they were dating but since they moved in together, she found herself to be a very domesticated woman, and she was enjoying it. Mike had not been this happy in a long time, things were really going well for the young couple and the best was yet to come. A baby, a marriage, and a career to be proud of, his only regret was that he had no family of his own to share it with. But Amy and Johnathan were his family now and that made him very proud.

Elizabeth was so busy she was surprised she had time to breathe. She associated her title of intern to 'person who does everything regardless of time, knowledge, or skill.' She knew her boss had confidence in her and she didn't want to let him, or herself, down. Their working relationship was excellent, he knew she was smart and gave her enough guidance to get her started on projects and then let her roll with them on her own. She always knew, however, that if she needed his help or support with a project, he'd be there. Her principal was a season – serving a huge purpose in her life now but once she moved on, she figured they'd never cross paths again.

Her parents were proud of her and complained that they never heard from her or saw her anymore but at this point her career was her priority and they'd just have to understand that. She would make it up to them somehow, sometime, but for now she remained focused on herself and her career.

Josh had tired of asking for time with her and being turned down every time so he ended the brief courtship with her which of course was fine with her, she kind of knew it was a matter of time. He had been a reason for sure, only in her life for a short period of time. Why? Maybe to remind her that she was still desirable? She didn't know and didn't waste any time thinking about it. She had way too much on her plate to worry about him.

Amy's sub was working out nicely, she had established a good rapport with the kids and her classroom management was that of a new teacher. She'd have to learn some lessons the hard way but Elizabeth could tell she'd be ok. She fit in well with her grade level team and the rest of the faculty and they all spoke fondly of Amy, they missed her.

The school staff had arranged a shower for Amy one day after school, most of which Elizabeth missed due to other duties but she'd been the one to get her there. She called her and said the sub couldn't find some of the math manipulatives and would she mind coming in to show her where she left them. Amy tried to explain where they were but Elizabeth shut her down immediately with a strong tone, "Aim I'm swamped, can you please just come in and show her after school next Thursday? She has to stay for a faculty meeting anyway so she'll be here." Elizabeth all but hung up on her to keep her from arguing and she felt bad but it had been her job to get Amy there for the shower.

She texted Mike the same day to let him in on the secret and he assured Elizabeth he'd be there afterward with his truck to lug all the goodies home. He was glad the school was handling the shower because quite honestly, he wouldn't have known the first thing to do to arrange one nor did he know anyone to solicit help from other than Elizabeth who was too busy to help anyway. Elizabeth had given the teachers who were planning the shower contact information for some of their other friends who weren't school affiliated so they'd be included as well.

Amy was overwhelmingly surprised when she arrived and became happily emotional when she realized she'd been duped. She really didn't expect a shower since Elizabeth was so busy and her mom was away and while she secretly wanted a shower as does every expectant mother, she accepted the fact that it wasn't going to happen. But then it did and she was touched.

Amy oohed and aahed as she opened each gift, making sure to have someone writing down whom to thank for each gift, and she must've said a hundred times as she opened gifts, "I can't wait for Mike to see this!" Someone was taking pictures, she was distinctly aware of the occasional flash. She stayed focused in the moment and couldn't stop talking and showing gifts to Mike when he showed up to help her get the shower gifts home.

With everything finally loaded in his truck, he leaned down to kiss Amy. "Just think," he said, "you'll have another shower in a few months for our wedding." They'd decided on November 11th for their wedding date, it would be a smaller event as weddings go, only one maid of honor, one bridesmaid, and two ushers. The invites would total about 100 people and they were both thrilled to be sharing this special day with their closest friends and family. Her parents said they'd book their flights once they were state-side for the birth of the baby, they hated doing anything online and they wanted Amy to help them with it. As Amy thought about these things and waved goodbye to Mike from her own car, she felt blessed beyond belief with the path her life was taking.

Saturday September 17th started like any other day, including the fact that Amy was still pregnant and not having labor pains. Ugh, she wondered, maybe it isn't really going to happen? Which was ludicrous, she knew it would, but she was so ready to have the baby and end the pregnancy. She and Mike had talked about having more kids, not anytime real soon but in the future and she had told him they'd have to plan it so that she wasn't pregnant over the hot summer months. He'd laughed at her but had often felt sorry for her as she appeared to be miserable with the combination of the extra weight and the heat. He was thrilled with all that was happening in his life and considered himself the luckiest man in the world.

Amy's parents were set to arrive on Monday and it still remained to be seen who would be welcoming who in regard to them and the baby. Amy had started to feel what she thought were contractions that morning but she wondered if a) they were in her imagination because she wanted to feel them so badly, or b) they were the Braxton-Hicks contractions she'd read about, which were false contractions. She didn't want to rush to the hospital only to have them send her back home because she wasn't ready. Mike panicked each time she moved suddenly or winced slightly, he planned to be in the delivery room with her but had no plans whatsoever to deliver the baby at home alone. While one was hesitant, the other was eager, and they often found themselves laughing at each other and at themselves. They were still so totally in love and couldn't wait to welcome their son.

Sunday came and went, and then Monday, the only interruption to the day being the arrival of Amy's parents. Mike had taken the day off. He refused to let Amy go to the airport alone and so the two of them went together in Mike's truck to pick her parents up.

At the sight of Amy, her mother placed her hands at her mouth and began to cry, Amy could tell by her stature but they were tears of happiness. They all hugged, Mike and Pete shook hands and exchanged pleasantries while Amy's mom doted on her daughter. She had a million questions and kept telling her how great she looked. Although she'd seen pictures along the way, seeing her in person was totally different and she loved every minute of it. "Pete, take our picture," she said shoving the camera she'd retrieved from her purse at her husband. He shuffled over to do as his wife requested. Lois hugged Amy closely and smiled for the camera.

They took a few more pictures of various groupings and were about to head to baggage claim when Amy cried out in what sounded like a cry of pain. Everyone turned to look at her and for a split second no one realized what might be happening. Mike was the first to react. "Amy, are you..." before he could finish she winced again and sunk down on the floor to her knees, holding her belly. This was it, she was in labor, and it was time to go welcome their son. Taking complete control, Mike rushed to Amy and supported her to a standing position while he simultaneously tossed his keys to Pete. "Get your bags and take my truck, white Ford 250, it's parked in lot C, spot #43, meet us at County General. We're taking a taxi."

It all happened so fast and while he didn't take the taxi for this reason, Mike was glad they'd done so, this way he could focus on Amy and not have to worry about driving. She seemed to be in a lot of pain by now, lying across the back seat with her head on Mike's lap, crying out and pulling her knees up in pain, then trying to extend her body as if it hurt less to be in a prone position. They were all over the backseat of the taxi and Mike was at a loss as to what to do other than rub her face and try to reassure her that this was normal. Was it? He had no idea but it was all he could think to say.

The taxi driver kept glancing nervously in the rearview mirror, it was obvious he was worried about childbirth happening in his taxi. He'd heard stories but

160

had never experienced it and he didn't want today to be the day he did. Amy's yelling continued and escalated, Mike couldn't help but feel sorry for the pain she was feeling and also a little guilty that he didn't have to bear any of it, but listening to her and watching her was not easy either. Mike saw the driver's concern and said "Don't worry, I'll tip you well." Tip or no tip, the driver did not want a birth happening in his back seat so he drove a little faster. Surely a cop would let him go under the circumstances.

The trip seemed to take forever and Amy's pain seemed to get worse. Sweat was beading on her forehead and she felt hot. Mike pulled out his cell phone and dialed 911. He alerted them that he was en route to the hospital with a nine-month pregnant woman in labor and could they please radio the hospital to have a medical team meet them at the door. He had to repeat it once as they couldn't hear him over Amy's yelling and crying. They asked him to hold while they relayed the information and then came back to him with instructions. Mike nodded and snapped the cell phone shut, not realizing they couldn't hear the nod, and then shouted to the driver, "Take us to the emergency room, they'll meet us there." The driver nodded and again accelerated the gas pedal even more, he'd be glad when this fare was over. "How much further?" Mike yelled over Amy's voice.

The driver looked as if he'd be just as happy parking the taxi and walking away but he replied, "Just a couple more blocks buddy, just a couple more blocks." And with that Amy began gasping for breath so quickly that it took Mike by surprise, he was startled, and continued talking to her.

"Amy we're almost there, hang on…we're almost there baby, I love you." As he tried to sooth her he reached for her face again and pulled his hand back suddenly, she was losing color. It caused him more concern than he already had, and he was about to say something to her when suddenly the yelling stopped, just like that. The silence was so deafening that the driver and Mike looked at each other in shock first, and then Mike looked down at Amy. With no color to her face at all, it appeared as if she'd passed out.

Fear encompassed Mike and he was at a loss for what to do. The driver might have been a little curious as to why the noise stopped but was more relieved than anything that it did. Mike shook Amy at her shoulders. "Amy, Amy. Amy wake up," he was saying.

The remainder of the ride, which amounted to about a minute and a half, continued this way with Mike trying to wake Amy up, unsuccessfully. The driver pulled the taxi under the emergency awning where he saw a gurney and three medical personnel waiting. The tires squealed but he made a perfect entry and Mike opened the door before the taxi stopped moving. When it did stop Mike jumped out and pointed to the backseat and then placed his hands on top of his head. "Help her, help her, she passed out about three or four minutes ago and she has no color to her, she looks like a ghost," he yelled. Truthfully he'd lost all track of time but he answered their questions as best he could. Nine months, due date was Saturday,

162

healthy pregnancy, first baby, no medicine that he was aware of, Dr. Beachy was her doctor, yes he was the father, and on and on they seemed to go. He wanted to yell at them to just take care of her but the truth was, they were.

During the interrogation they had moved from the taxi to a patient room in the emergency ward and things were happening quickly. Doctors and nurses were rushing and he kept getting pushed from side to side, it seemed that no matter where he stood he was in someone's way. They were yelling things, medical things that he didn't understand, they gave her a shot, they placed an oxygen mask over her face but she had yet to show any signs of waking up. He had questions and did ask a few but no one would answer him, they were too busy talking to each other about what to do, stats, levels, and did anyone call Dr. Beachy yet.

With all that was happening it became obvious to Mike that this was something very serious, not normal at all, and suddenly he was scared, more scared than he'd ever been in any of the encounters he'd had in Iraq or Afghanistan. The events of the next few minutes happened quickly. Machines started beeping, voices were accelerating, people started rushing, he was being pushed more and more, and the next thing he knew a nurse had him by the arms pulling him out the door. "Sir you're going to have to wait out here, we have to do our work and we can't have you in the way. One of us will come and fill you in as soon as possible but for now you'll need to wait out here." Mike would've sworn his feet were glued to the floor but this tiny nurse had no trouble whatsoever shuffling him out to the waiting room.

As she shut the door on him he stood there dumbfounded. He vaguely heard voices behind him and as he turned he realized he was in the waiting room with others, some waiting to be seen, some waiting for their loved ones who were being seen, and across the room coming in through the glass sliding doorway were Amy's parents, all smiles as they walked toward Mike and those smiles didn't diminish until they got closer to him and saw the look on his face. It was fallen, glazed over, as if in shock. Lois grabbed his arms, "Mike what's wrong, oh my God what's wrong? Is it Amy? Is it the baby? What's gone wrong, oh my God," and she turned to her husband as his arms instinctively came out to embrace her.

Mike continued staring, he didn't know what to say, mainly because he didn't know what was wrong and therefore didn't know what to tell them. He'd just been shoved out into the waiting room with no explanation. Pete hugged his now crying wife and asked Mike the same question, "What's wrong, son?" Mike pulled himself together enough to tell them he didn't know.

They all moved toward chairs around the corner, out of sight of most, and sat down as Mike explained what had happened, first in the taxi and then in the emergency room. As he was talking a doctor came out of the exam room area and headed toward them. Pete saw him first and fixated his gaze on the doctor. Seeing Pete's reaction, Mike turned and looked too and he immediately stood up, asking the doctor what was going on. The doctor asked him, "You're Amy's husband?" Mike responded that he was the baby's father which prompted the doctor to ask, "Who is her next of kin?"

Lois immediately broke into uncontrollable sobs as Pete addressed the doctor. "We're her parents but Mike has every right to speak on Amy's behalf and know what's going on." The doctor nodded slightly and turned toward Mike.

"The baby is on its way, Amy is ready to deliver, and the baby is in good shape to deliver naturally, but Amy is in distress. We don't know what's wrong or what's happened. Dr. Beachy is on his way. We've reviewed her records, there isn't anything indicating why this should be happening, she was in good health. Did anything happen right before she went into labor? Anything at all?"

Mike and Pete both shook their heads, Lois couldn't, she was crying too hard, her baby, who was having a baby, was in distress and there was nothing she could do about it. The doctor spoke next, "OK, let me get in there and see what's happening, I promise we'll keep you updated" and he started to walk away as Mike yelled after him.

"Can't I come in with you? Please Doctor, I really want to be with her, please," he pleaded and the doctor had a difficult time looking him in the eyes.

"I don't think that's a good idea Mike," and with that he walked away. The three returned to their chairs. Lois couldn't stop crying and Mike wasn't sure how much longer he himself would be able to hold it together. He thought about asking a receptionist if there was a private room or a chapel they could go to but he didn't want to leave the waiting room in case they came looking for him. With good news, that's why they'd want him, he thought, for good news. But now he was scared. Amy was in distress. He'd been with soldiers in the field who were hurt and he'd heard the medics use that term, 'in distress' and he knew the end result wasn't good in most of those cases but this was different, they were here in the hospital with all the support needed to make everything ok. Amy would deliver the baby and then they'd get whatever was wrong with her straightened out and in a few more days they'd be back in their apartment and Lois would be rocking her grandson. Yes, a few more days and all would be back to normal, he just needed to get through this first.

What seemed like hours was in reality no more than 30 minutes when Dr. Beachy came out to the waiting room. He wasn't smiling, but didn't doctors always do that? Come out poker-faced to keep you wondering until they could share the news? He hoped so, God he hoped so. As he approached them all three stood to face him. They didn't need words; he knew what they wanted to know so he spoke as soon as he was within a close proximity to them.

"Hi Mike, and I assume you're Amy's parents?" he said toward Pete and Lois who nodded affirmatively. There were no handshakes, no time for pleasantries. They wanted to know what was happening. Dr. Beachy spoke immediately. "We went ahead and delivered the baby Mike, your son is fine, 7 pounds 4 ounces, 20 inches long, healthy and breathing well, congratulations."

He paused, which was his mistake as all three jumped in asking about Amy with worried faces and voices. The joy of waiting for a child or grandchild had been diminished, there was no joy at the moment, only worry for Amy. Dr. Beachy bit his lip and looked at the family members. He inhaled and exhaled loudly. "I'm sorry, we don't know what happened," he said scratching his head, "she was healthy just last week when I examined her but I'm sorry, she didn't make it. We lost her a few minutes ago. We did everything humanly possible…" and from there the words were just noise.

None of the three heard anything he said. Lois fell into Pete's arms, sobbing uncontrollably, Pete broke down and started crying, and Mike began yelling out 'no, no, no' as he too began welling up with tears. What could have happened? What went wrong? Was it something he did? His emotions were that of pain and anger, he'd never felt like this before. The next thing he heard the doctor saying was, "…of course we'd like to perform an autopsy to find out what went wrong. I've asked a nurse to find you a private place to wait until we clean things up and then you can see her if you'd like. You can see the baby anytime you want. Again, I'm sorry Mike," as he placed his hand on Mike's shoulder and offered a nod toward Lois and Pete as he didn't even know their names.

And just like that he walked back into the exam room area, leaving them alone in the waiting room as onlookers whispered amongst themselves, offered sympathetic looks toward them, and turned back away from them as life went on. For everyone except Amy. Life was moving on without her. None of the three understood and it wasn't fair. The nurse came out shortly afterward and ushered them to a private room off the exam room area. All three were still crying although Lois had settled down a little, Mike believed she was probably in shock, he thought they all were to an extent. The fact that Amy was gone was just unbelievable and without realizing it, the baby was the last thing on any of their minds. No one even thought about poor little Johnathan Michael who would never meet his mother. They were already grieving their loss of Amy.

The next hour passed slowly, painfully, as they waited for word that they could go see Amy. Mike wasn't sure how he'd handle it in front of Pete and Lois and planned to ask to go in alone. He had no idea why but Elizabeth popped into his mind and he wondered if he should call her. She was Amy's best friend and of course would need to know, but did she need to know now? He asked Lois what she thought and she shrugged her shoulders, nothing seemed to matter to anyone right now. Deciding against it, he sat back in his chair and waited.

Moments later a nurse came in and told them they could come back to see her now if they wanted to. She told them there would be someone here to help them with procedures after they spent their time with Amy, to answer questions about what to do next, who to call and how to get Amy's body to the proper place. Amy's body. Mike felt his anger rise as this stranger referred to the love of his life as a body. He clenched his fists and tilted his head downward, he knew she was only doing her job and that Amy was only a dead body to her, but to him she was everything. He suggested Pete and Lois go in first, he said he'd wait and go alone after them, and once they left the room he sat down in the chair, put his head in his hands, and cried like he'd never cried before. He had a healthy son and Amy was gone. As he reflected, he tried to remember the pain he'd felt when he lost his parents, and then his grandparents and then soldiers through the act of war. They had all affected him emotionally but nothing he could recall even came close to the pain he was feeling in his heart right now.

Chapter Twelve

"Be slow to fall into friendship; but when thou art in, continue firm & constant." – Socrates

The next few days were a blur. Amy's parents had offered to take care of all of the arrangements for the services, they'd had a small life insurance policy on Amy since she was little and felt it was their obligation to do it. Mike didn't disagree but did offer his help in whatever way they felt they needed it.

The call to Elizabeth was one of the most difficult calls he'd ever had to make, how do you tell someone who answers the phone with the greeting, "Is Johnathan Michael here?" that her best friend has just passed away? Elizabeth was grief stricken. She went through the motions at work but felt like a part of her was missing, she'd never lost anyone she'd been as close to as she had Amy, not even Lance. She called her parents to tell them and they cried too, they had loved Amy like a second daughter and had asked about the baby, who would take care of him? Elizabeth responded that of course Mike would, he was the baby's father. During their conversation her mom had said that Amy had been a good season for Elizabeth.

Elizabeth smiled as a tear fell down her cheek recalling her recent thought about Amy being her lifetime. She reminded her mother that Amy didn't buy into all of that but she agreed it had been a great season, one she wouldn't have changed for a million dollars. She felt like Amy had had such a positive impact on her life and she would forever be grateful for that.

Mike took the baby home on Wednesday and was tied to the apartment with him. He had no clue how to take care of a baby and no desire to be in the apartment he'd shared with Amy but Amy's parents were busy with funeral arrangements and Elizabeth was working 14 hour days. A few of Amy's friends would drop by to extend their condolences, most of whom Mike didn't know, and to him they were just an intrusion. He knew they meant well but he was still in a state of shock from the events of the past few days. Lois and Pete had gotten a hotel room, they'd only seen the baby once in the hospital. Mike hoped that once the funeral was over they'd come over and offer to stay with the baby for a while, he needed some time to himself. This had been a whirlwind for him, gaining a newborn and losing his soon-to-be-wife all in one day was overwhelming at best and he hoped he could keep it together. The nurses had been very kind at the hospital, trying to give him crash courses in diapering, feeding, burping, bathing, and all the other things he'd need to do for his son. A friend of Amy's had brought him a book about taking care of your newborn but he just couldn't bring himself to read it. He did what he thought was right and a few times he had called Lois who talked him through what he needed to know. She stayed in touch with Mike throughout the week and kept him abreast of the service which was scheduled for Saturday, this way teachers who had worked with Amy could attend and not have to miss work.

On Saturday the Church was filled with friends who all came to mourn the loss of such a young life. Lois had done a very nice job of creating the kind of environment Amy would've approved of, nice without being overdone. Elizabeth had planned to eulogize her friend but at the last minute said she couldn't do it, she was too emotional and didn't want to ruin the service. Lois, Pete, Mike and Elizabeth sat in the front row, Lois and Pete wanted it that way, and Johnathan slept in Mike's arms throughout the entire service. They had placed a picture of Johnathan in the casket before closing it, they all thought Amy would've liked that.

The preacher spoke very eloquently about a woman he'd never met and before they knew it they were leaving the cemetery, it had all gone by so quickly. People were asking to see the baby, expressing their sympathies along with their congratulations. For the few who asked to hold him, Mike was only too happy to let them. He loved his son but being a full-time parent was tiring and he had no idea how single parents did it as he thought about Gina, the single mom who'd worked with Amy at the Carriage House. He was relieved for the short breaks.

Lois and Pete spent a little time with Johnathan but not as much as Mike would've expected. He supposed that maybe the baby reminded them too much of Amy and if he had asked them, that's exactly what they would've told him, but he didn't ask.

Elizabeth had arranged to use the school cafeteria for the gathering after the burial and about 100 people had attended. Pete and Lois spent the time meeting colleagues of Amy's. Mike was shocked to overhear them tell a few of the teachers that they planned to head back to Germany early next week. Their daughter had only been gone since Monday, today was Saturday, not even a whole week and they were ready to leave. Plus they'd spent literally no quality time with Johnathan. Mike was confused and thought perhaps he'd misheard so he approached them later after everyone had left and they were heading to their vehicles. Mike was carrying Johnathan and held him out toward Lois. "Do you want to hold him a little, Lois?" Mike asked with as much enthusiasm as he could muster.

Lois pulled away, "No, not now Mike, I think I'm coming down with a cold. Must be the change in weather from Germany to here. It's cooler over there right now you know and I think the warmer air here must've affected me."

Mike pulled the baby back. He continued the conversation, "So how long do you think you'll stay here? You're welcome to stay at the apartment for as long as you want. You could have our, I'm sorry, I mean my room, I'll take the couch."

Lois looked at Pete and nudged him gently on the arm. When he looked at her she tilted her head toward Mike, as if she was urging Pete to do something. Pete hesitated and then let out a sigh.

"Mike we're going to be heading back to Germany come Tuesday. This weather is really getting to Lois, as she said, and, well, we just need to get back. Elizabeth helped us book our flights a few days ago so we'll be out of your hair Tuesday. We hope you'll stay in touch though…" and with that Mike stopped walking and just stared at Amy's parents. He didn't stop to think, the words just came out.

"Stay in touch? Are you kidding me with this?" he said, almost yelling. Lois and Pete had stopped walking too and stared at Mike in disbelief that he was shocked by their announcement. "I mean, are you kidding me? Your daughter has been gone less than a week, you have a grandson you haven't held for more than 5 minutes, and you need to get back to Germany? Why? Why? You don't work, it's not like you have things to take care of over there that can't wait, do you? I mean come on, level with me, what's really going on here? I'm dying trying to take care of this baby on my own," he said as he hoisted the baby a little. The term 'dying' had been lost on him but not on Lois and Pete and Lois got teary-eyed yet again and started walking away toward their rental car.

Pete stepped up and put his arm around Mike's shoulder and began walking him toward his own truck. "Mike, we're sorry, we just aren't handling this well. We just lost the only child we ever had. We don't understand what happened, why Amy, well, you know, we just don't understand. And being here around you, around the baby, well, it's just too hard on Lois. Look at her, she's still in a state of shock, Amy was our only child and she's just not adjusting well." Mike just

174

stared at him and Pete continued. "Listen, you two weren't married, we know you have no obligation to stay in touch with us, but we hope you will. Maybe one day Lois will be ready to be in Johnathan's life but right now, I'm not even sure she's acknowledging that he exists Mike, and that's not good for a baby. A baby needs people around it who love it and want to be in its life and right now, as sad as it is, that's not Lois."

Mike could only stare, he couldn't find the words, and he wondered what Amy would say if she could speak to him right now. What would she tell him to do? He came up with nothing and with nothing left to say, Pete went back to Lois and escorted her to their car. After putting her in the passenger seat, he walked around to the driver's side, got in, started the car and drove off leaving Mike standing with his son in the parking lot. Mike watched, staring at the tail lights in disbelief, unsure of what to do. He looked up toward the sky, imagining Amy looking down on him and their son. He wondered to himself, Amy, what happened? How in God's name was he going to do this? He had no idea, but he knew he had to try, for Amy's sake.

The Army had given Mike 30 days of emergency leave under the circumstances. His command had been very understanding of the situation and he felt fortunate for that, he knew of others that wouldn't have been. He wasn't necessarily excited about being a 24/7 daddy for the next 30 days but he was planning on trying to get some things in order. He assumed he'd need a daycare provider for Johnathan and there were follow-up doctor appointments. Almost everything he did diverted his thoughts to a memory of Amy. God he missed her. He found himself talking to her throughout the day, mostly asking for guidance and advice and sometimes getting angry and cursing her for leaving him and not being there for him and Johnathan. He knew it wasn't the child's fault but he never planned on parenting alone. It was much more difficult than he could've imagined with nightly feedings, crying spells, and smells from diapers that would've put some of his soldiers to shame. He had so much to learn, he was certain he'd mess the baby up before he turned one. Someone had recommended he read a book about what to expect during the first year of life but he wasn't sure he wanted to know what was coming, it might scare him too much.

Every day he stumbled upon at least one new thing he didn't know before, usually more than one and that was enough learning for him. Elizabeth stopped by the Saturday following the funeral. She'd stayed in touch with him by text since the funeral and she helped him as much as she could but when it came to baby questions she knew even less than he did. Some of his soldier's wives had come over and offered to help, cook, babysit, whatever he needed, but he didn't like to socialize on a personal level with his soldiers and he thought it might be crossing a line. He reminded himself that he could quickly promote again in a few short years and he wanted to walk the straight and narrow. All he had was Elizabeth and her time, as well as her ability to help him with the baby, was extremely limited. Elizabeth plopped down on the couch after hugging Mike in the doorway. "So how are you doing?" she asked him. He didn't look good. He looked worn down and tired. He had bags under his eyes, she'd never noticed those before.

He ran his hands through his hair and sighed. "Ah, Elizabeth, you have no idea. I'm such a mixture of emotions right now and more than that I'm at a total loss for how to take care of my son. Nothing comes naturally to me, he cries and I have no idea what's wrong with him and of course he can't tell me, I have no one to call to help me, and I'm going stir-crazy in this apartment. Everything reminds me of Amy, there's nowhere I can go to just relax and take a few breaths, and Elizabeth I love my son but I swear he has Amy's eyes and just looking at him makes me think I'm looking at her. God it hurts so much. I miss her so much."

Elizabeth listened carefully, she missed her friend too, horribly, and she knew the pain Mike spoke of as she felt it too. She reached her arm out to Mike's shoulder with a look of sympathy on her face. Yes she was hurting too but Mike's whole world had been turned upside down in a matter of minutes two weeks ago. She wasn't sure where the words came from but there they were.

"Go," she said and nodded toward the door. Mike just looked at her with a look of confusion.

"Go where?" he asked.

"Anywhere you want Mike, just go, I'll stay here with Johnathan. Just tell me what time he needs to be fed and where the diapers are, I'll take it from there." Mike's head startled in surprised, and then he started laughing. He laughed so hard that Elizabeth starting laughing too. "What?" she asked, "What's so funny?"

Still laughing Mike said between gasps of laughter, "You, taking care of, the baby, me leaving, you, feeding the baby, you..." Elizabeth reached out and whacked his arm.

"Hey, I'm trying to do a nice thing for you, trying to give you a little bit of a break, now tell me what I need to know and go. I'll be fine. If I need to I'll call my mom to come over. He's sleeping now, right? How long will he sleep?" Mike's chuckles slowed down enough for him to respond in a normal tone.

"You're serious?" Mike asked her and she nodded. "OK, he should be good for another two hours, then he'll need to be fed. The bottles are ready in the fridge, give him the blue one. Warm it for about 15 seconds first in the microwave. I'll try to be back before then but just in case I'm not."

She stood up and so did he as she began pushing him toward the door. "Go. I'll be fine. Stay out all day if you want, I'll be fine."

Mike reached for his keys and walked toward the door, Elizabeth following behind him, and then he said with a smile, "It's not you I'm worried about, it's my son." Elizabeth smiled back at him.

"Go!" she said, and with that Mike was out the door. Elizabeth pushed it shut and turned around to face the apartment, leaning against the door. She saw the baby monitor on the end table, the red light illuminated indicating she'd hear Johnathan when he woke up. And then it hit her. What had she just done?

Mike stayed away from the house for about four hours. He texted Elizabeth about every 20 minutes the first two hours but soon realized she was ok, or at least she was pretending to be. He ended up going over to a buddy's house. His friend was surprised to see him and eagerly invited him in to have a few beers. Married with three kids of his own, he couldn't imagine what Mike was going through being alone with a newborn, he felt for him. They talked a little about Amy and the baby but for the most part the conversation was about Army stuff and sports. They'd each had three beers when Mike said he'd better be leaving. He chuckled as he explained that he'd left Johnathan alone with a woman who knew less about kids than he did. His friend laughed and assured him that childcare came naturally to women. Mike thanked him and said goodbye and headed back toward the apartment.

For the first time in two weeks he felt good, really good, normal. He felt a sense of relief that he hadn't felt since before Amy died. He was disappointed to find that the feeling started to diminish as reality got closer and closer, block by block. He tried to recall the conversations he'd had from his friend, thinking they would rejuvenate the feeling of happiness, but all he could recall were diapers and bottles.

The second Mike walked out the door Elizabeth nearly turned and yanked the door open to call him back. She had no idea where her burst of kindness (more like insanity) came from to have offered to stay with a baby for more than two minutes let alone several hours. She thought twice and decided to let Mike go but she'd call her mom, her mom loved babies and wouldn't mind coming over to help. She went to her purse and reached for her cell and punched the auto-dial for Mom and Dad. They didn't have cell phones, they only had the land line and she waited not-so-patiently as it rang. The baby hadn't stirred at all but she panicked more and more with each passing moment.

She looked around the apartment as she waited and couldn't help thinking about Amy, everything in the apartment had Amy's touch and it made her sad, sad to the point of tearing up. "Dad, hey, I need to talk to mom." She could imagine her father standing in the kitchen holding the receiver to his ear.

"Well it's nice to hear your voice too honey, how are you?" Not now, Elizabeth thought.

"I'm fine dad, now can I please talk to mom?" He noticed the anxiousness in her voice then and thought it best not to agitate her.

"Well your mom's gone over to Daniel's for the day, she's watching the kids. You know she can't get enough of those grandkids. Anything I can do for you, sweetheart?" She didn't mind that her dad used those pet names for her, she was his only daughter so she allowed him this but she rolled her eyes just the same at his offer of help.

"No dad, its fine, thanks, bye."

"Love you honey," she heard him say as she snapped the phone shut. Now what, she thought to herself, mom can't help me.

She looked around the apartment as if she were looking for answers. She looked again at the baby monitor, it hadn't moved, and then she realized how ridiculous that thought was and she laughed out loud. She moved toward the monitor and picked it up. She knew enough to know how these worked so she jokingly placed it up to her lips and spoke into it, "Johnathan, if you stay asleep until your daddy gets home I'll give you a million dollars." And then she laughed again at herself.

She glanced around quickly to assure no one was watching her act this way, of course there wasn't and she found herself wondering if Amy was watching. She sat down on the nearby recliner, still holding the monitor, and had a silent conversation with Amy. She hadn't planned on it, it just seemed to come naturally. She asked her friend why she had to die and leave them all, especially her beautiful baby boy. She asked her how in the world Mike was supposed to make it all work, he had a heart of gold but was clueless in his new role. And she asked her how she was supposed to get through the rough days, who was she going to call, and who was going to encourage her and keep her motivated. She found tears streaming down her cheeks as she talked with her friend. In her mind Amy answered each question. While it was Elizabeth posing the responses in her own mind, she found that she wasn't hearing the answers she wanted to.

181

She'd been there for over an hour, deep in thought, and it startled her when the baby monitor she was still holding started making sounds. She glared at it with a quizzical look and realized it wasn't the monitor, it was Johnathan. She sat still, barely breathing, as if he'd go back to sleep if he didn't hear her. Nope, that wasn't happening, he kept whimpering and eventually started letting out staccato little bursts of noises. She couldn't call it screaming or crying, just these noises she couldn't really describe.

Before she knew it she'd pushed herself up off the chair and was heading toward the baby's room, monitor still in hand. She hadn't seen it since it'd been decorated and now she felt guilty that she hadn't taken the time to do so, it probably would've meant a lot to Amy. As she entered the room and looked around, she found her feet frozen in place, her mouth hung open in awe. Amy had decorated the room in the jungle theme they'd briefly discussed, complete with a beautiful hand-painted mural on one of the walls. As soon as she saw it she knew the mural had to be Amy's work, she could feel the love she'd poured into it. She looked around the rest of the room. There was a changing table with a little blanket over the padding, jungle themed. There was a rocking chair in the corner, most likely a place Amy had expected to spend a lot of time feeding her son and rocking him to sleep. A crib occupied most of the far wall, a jungle animal mobile hung above it. She knew Johnathan was in it, the mattress was raised really high and she could see him lying on it, still making his noises. In another corner there were some shelves, with a lamp in the shape of a jungle tree, jungle animals dancing on the lightshade.

Taking it all in, she moved toward the wall with the mural, it had a lot of trees, and when she reached it she placed her hand upon it and rubbed across the gray smiling elephant that was facing her. So smooth, so colorful, so beautiful, all for this little boy. As she ran her hand across the mural, across the tiger with his stripes of black, across the lion with his non-ferocious roaring look, she came to the border of the mural and her eyes moved downward where she saw a black scribble in the corner. Was it a spider? No, not in this perfect jungle. Moving closer she saw that it was an inscription. Kneeling down to put herself at eye level with the writing, she saw a recent date. And then she read the words, 'Johnathan Michael, You are my lifetime. Love, Mommy."

Johnathan had continued making his noises the whole time she was viewing the mural and now she joined him. Sobs racked her whole body as she knelt at the writing, she had to brace herself against the wall to keep her balance. Her heart physically hurt and she clutched at it, she'd never felt like this before. The simple words that probably would've made others smile had more meaning to her than anyone would ever know. Amy *did* buy into the philosophy that Elizabeth and her mother lived by. Johnathan's noises grew louder and she knew she had to pull herself together for his sake. For Amy's sake. For all their sakes.

Crossing the room toward the crib, she looked in at the newborn and cocked her head sideways.

Reaching in once, and then pulling her hands back, she reached in a second time. Why did this feel so awkward to her? Slowly she placed her hands on the sides of the baby and lifted. His trunk came toward her but his head and legs hung below. She quickly put him back down and tried again from a different angle. This time she slid one hand under his head and neck and used the other one to support his back and legs, he wasn't that big, and before she knew it she had him up to her chest. She rested the baby against herself and began patting his back. Was this what you were supposed to do? She'd never, ever held a baby this young, her nieces and nephews were at least six months old before she'd picked them up. Without knowing it she started bouncing her legs to provide a little rhythm and movement for the baby. It was working, he was calming down a little bit.

What was it Mike had said about a bottle, it was blue, heat it up or something, why hadn't she listened better? But then Mike said he'd try to be back before the two hours was up, but he wasn't, and she was going to have to do something.

Carrying Johnathan, she walked out toward the kitchen. Once again everything she saw reminded her of Amy. She moved toward the fridge and was caught off guard again when she noticed the pictures attached to the fridge with magnets. One was of her and Mike at the beach but there were three of the two girls; one at the beach, one at the Carriage House, and one at school. In all three pictures the girls looked happy, relaxed, fun, alive. Yes, in those pictures they were both alive, and now one of them wasn't. Shaking it from her mind she opened the refrigerator door and reached for the blue bottle. Mike's refrigerator shelves were nearly empty. She thought people showered you with food when a loved one died but clearly that wasn't the case here.

The microwave was right beside the fridge. Juggling the baby and the bottle she managed to open it, put the bottle in, and set it for, what was it Mike had said it was supposed to be, 15 seconds? Hitting the start button, she walked around the kitchen with Johnathan, he was still making some noises but nothing too loud or bothersome so he must be ok. "So Mr. Johnathan, I am your Aunt Elizabeth and guess what? I love you. I love you very much, and you know what else? You have an awesome mom who loves you too, more than anything, and she couldn't wait to meet you." She paused for a second. "Your mom would be so proud of you Johnathan, and I know you're going to grow up to make everyone else proud. You know why I know that Johnathan? Because you are Amy Michelle Wenger's little boy and that alone makes you awesome."

'Ding' went the microwave. Elizabeth moved toward it, opened it, and carefully pulled the bottle out. Wasn't she supposed to test it on her arm or something? She'd come this far, she didn't want to mess it up now. Mike hadn't said anything about testing it so she went to sit in the recliner in the living room, she just couldn't bring herself to sit in the rocker intended for Amy, and she placed Johnathan in the crook of her left arm. When she had him positioned where she wanted him, she lifted the bottle to his

185

mouth. His tiny, soft, pink lips molded around the nipple of the bottle and he started to suck. Elizabeth watched in wonderment, she'd never been this close to a newborn, or any baby, taking his bottle. His little lips pursed on the bottle, she couldn't take her eyes off of him. How did he know what to do? Instinct, she assumed, instinct. Amazing, she thought.

And then her eyes popped wide open. Wait a minute, she'd never done this before, and she'd never been around to watch anyone who'd done it, so how did she know how and what to do? She knew the answer before she asked herself the question. It was instinct, and she smiled, pleased with herself as she settled back into the recliner to feed Amy and Mike's son.

Chapter Thirteen

"The ornament of a house is the friends who frequent it." - Ralph Waldo Emerson

Mike walked in just as Johnathan was sucking down the last of the bottle. He stopped and stared. "I thought I'd be home in time for the feeding, I'm sorry Elizabeth," he apologized and then moved toward them.

Elizabeth smiled. "We're fine, we did great, didn't we Johnathan?" she asked him in an infantile voice as she nuzzled her face toward his.

"Whoa," Mike said in amazement, "I'm shocked! Never expected to see this, thought I'd meet you running out the door," he said with a laugh as he reached to take his son from her. She lifted Johnathan toward Mike, who took him in his big strong hands with ease. "Did you burp him yet?"

Elizabeth stood and faced them. "Um, you didn't say anything about burping him." Mike laughed again.

"So that would be a no. No worries, I'll do it," and he took her place in the recliner. As he rocked and burped the baby, they chatted comfortably. Mike shared the conversation he'd had with Amy's parents the week before in the school parking lot. Elizabeth was surprised but not shocked, mainly because she could relate to the lack of emotional feelings toward a baby, although her reasons were very different than Lois and Pete's. He told her he had 30 days of leave which he'd already told her before but she didn't deem it important to point that out. She could only imagine what his life was like.

Having similar lives that were career oriented, she couldn't imagine having a baby thrown into it. She asked him what his plan was after his 30 days of emergency leave were up and he said he had no idea. He planned to use the 30 days to figure it out but so far, he'd come up with nothing. They talked about school, about Amy's sub and the fact that she was doing great and they'd probably give her Amy's contract, and Elizabeth told him how much she was enjoying the administrative skills she was learning. She glanced at her watch then and said she'd better get going, she had a ton of work to do but she made sure to tell Mike how good it was to see him, and to be sure to call her if he needed anything. Mike said he would and hugged her good-bye. Elizabeth went out the door to freedom while Mike closed the door to it.

The next two weeks at school were the busiest two weeks of Elizabeth's life. She worked morning to night and then went to college Monday and Wednesday evenings. With the internship in place she'd had to give up the TA job but she didn't care, the internship would be much more beneficial in the long run. She barely had time to stop and eat and often didn't take the time. She was losing weight but when her mother showed up at school one day with two take-out meals from the Carriage House, Elizabeth felt forced to take time for lunch. She would say she felt obligated to stop and eat the meal her mother had brought her but the truth was she would've given anything for a reason to sit down for any period of time, no matter how short it was. Right now, Mark's famous club sandwich with a side of coleslaw and fries was like a feast to her.

She and her mother made small talk the first few minutes and her mother shared her concern regarding Elizabeth working so much, she was worried she'd get sick and wondered how she ever expected to meet a man when she was at the school all the time. Here we go again, Elizabeth thought, more talk about me finding a man. Why didn't her mother understand that that wasn't important to her? Not now, and possibly not ever.

Elizabeth quickly changed the subject and told her mother that she'd been spending any free time, which was extremely limited, with Johnathan and Mike. She told her the milestones she'd been reaching with the baby, first feeding him-without help she added- then diapering, and most recently, she'd bathed him. Mike was right there telling her how to do it but she did it. Her mother listened in amazement, she couldn't believe this was her daughter, the one who'd shunned her nieces and nephews until they were practically five years old (okay, that was an exaggeration), the one who had antagonized her for years by telling her she didn't want children of her own, here she was bragging about how she took care of someone else's baby. Elizabeth knew her mother well and read the look on her face.

"Mom, don't get excited, I'm not going to go have more grandkids for you. You know I'm in love with my career and that's my priority and by the number of hours I'm working now, I could never have a kid that I was responsible for, it'd starve to death because I'd never be home to feed it. Speaking of which, I don't think I've fed my fish in a month," she laughed, "but I have to tell you Mom, it's not as bad as I thought it would be. I really enjoy spending time with Johnathan. I mean, I know I can come and go when I want and I don't have to put up with the crying all night long and if the diaper's too bad I just tell Mike I'm leaving, but I'm kind of shocked at how much I don't hate it."

She took a breath then while her mother absorbed all that she'd said, and then smiled. "Now what are you smiling at Mom, you did hear me say I'm not going to go have a kid, didn't you?"

The smile never left her mother's face as she replied, "I heard you Elizabeth. I heard you loud and clear. Now tell me, what has Mike decided to do, does he have arrangements made for when his emergency leave is up?" Elizabeth sighed heavily and pushed her plate away.

"Well he signed him up for a daycare on post. A month old and that poor baby has to spend most of his day with strangers. I feel sorry for him, and I know Amy is probably turning over in her grave, but he really doesn't have a choice. He has to work." Her mom listened and nodded. She wondered if she should offer to help out but decided not to, she wasn't sure why, she just didn't. "He applied for a school in Kansas that starts in January," she continued.

"He's still considering that?" her mother asked with a raised voice? "I thought he'd give that idea up under the circumstances."

Elizabeth nodded. "I thought so too, and it's not my place to say that to him but he did mention that he's moving forward with it. He's determined to have a successful career and not to let anything get in his way, he hasn't made any changes to his plans since the baby came and Amy left. I don't know how he thinks he'll do it but he says he will." Both women picked up their sodas to take a drink but Elizabeth sat hers down quickly when she realized the time. "Mom I have to go, we've been sitting here over an hour and I'm going to get fired."

Her mom wiped her hands on her napkin and stood nodding. "I understand honey, just please take care of yourself, don't overdo it, and let us know if you need anything. And Elizabeth? Your dad and I are just so darn proud of you, we hope you know that." Elizabeth smiled and nodded, hugged her mother, and nearly ran out of her office to tend to the rest of her agenda for the day. It had been a much needed break and she was thankful her mother had taken the time to do it.

Mike went back to work as expected on the Monday that his 30 day leave ended. He'd dropped

Johnathan off at the daycare and had listed Elizabeth as an emergency contact but then realized he hadn't asked her first. Pulling out his cell as he drove away from the daycare, he pressed her number and hoped she'd answer. She shouldn't be too busy yet, it was only 6 AM, that was the earliest the day care would take Johnathan, and she picked up on the first ring. After assuring her nothing was wrong he asked her if it would be ok if he listed her as the emergency contact at the daycare. She assumed it was just like at her school, they only call the emergency contact person when they can't reach the parent. Then that person gets in touch with the parent and tells them to call the school, nothing to it, sure, put her down. Mike thanked her and asked her to wish him luck on his first day back, which she did.

It was nearly 6:30 PM when her cell rang next. She looked at the screen at the unknown number. She considered ignoring it, she still had some loose ends to tie up at school and she had night class at seven but she decided to pick up. Listening carefully to the caller, she learned it was the daycare where Johnathan was enrolled. The director informed her that they closed half an hour ago and Johnathan's father hadn't yet picked him up. They'd tried to contact him by cell but he wasn't answering. She was listed as the emergency contact and would she please be able to come pick him up.

Elizabeth panicked. This wasn't what she'd bargained for when she agreed to be the emergency contact and her first thought was that she didn't have a car seat in her car. She asked if she could have a few minutes to try and reach Mike but the supervisor replied with an irritated tone that they'd already waited half an hour and they had to leave themselves. Without much choice, Elizabeth said she'd be right there.

Fortunately for her, the school district had given all the administrators, including interns, car stickers to get onto post so she would be permitted to get in through the guarded gate. She asked the Director for the address, punched it into her cell phone's GPS and headed out the door. She still had the problem of a car seat but she'd figure that out when she got there and she'd yell at Mike later.

On her way there she texted a friend from her night class and asked her to tell her professor she'd be late, that she had a slight emergency but she'd be there. Then she focused her attention on getting to the day care.

The director was standing in the lobby holding Johnathan and a clipboard when Elizabeth walked in and she didn't look happy to say the least. She shoved the clipboard toward Elizabeth and asked her to sign. Elizabeth couldn't help feeling as if she was signing for a package delivery, then the Director proceeded to remind Elizabeth that there is a one dollar charge per minute for every minute past six that Johnathan is picked up. She also mentioned something about this not being a good impression to make on the first day. Elizabeth informed her that she had no idea what had happened but she was sure there was a valid reason, and then she apologized and assured her it wouldn't happen again. And she certainly hoped it wouldn't.

The irritated director took the clipboard back with a somewhat disgusted look and handed Elizabeth the baby and the diaper bag. Now the transaction is complete, Elizabeth thought. How could a woman like this work in a day care, she wondered?

Nearly pushing Elizabeth and the baby out the door, Elizabeth heard the click of the lock behind her. Great, she thought, now what. "Oh shit," she said aloud, "a car seat." She turned around to see if the daycare might have one she could borrow but the lights were already out and Miss Pleasant was nowhere in sight. Now what? Think Elizabeth, think. She sat down on the step, holding Johnathan in one arm and pulling out her cell. She called Mike, no answer. She tried again, no answer. This time she left a message, "Mike, it's Elizabeth, not sure where you are or what's going on but I have Johnathan, the day care called and apparently they close at six, which means you have to pick him up by six. Anyway, we're sitting at the daycare and I have no car seat and don't know what else to do. Hope you get this message and call me soon." She clicked the phone off and stared at it, willing Mike to call her back immediately.

Not knowing what else to do she called her mother. She explained the situation and asked her if she still had a car seat in the garage that she used to cart the grandkids around. Her mother said she did but she couldn't get onto post. Thinking quickly, Elizabeth told her mother to meet her at the Carriage House, it was right outside the post. She knew it was illegal and very unsafe to drive with the baby and no car seat but she didn't see any alternative, she'd have to drive to the Carriage House holding Johnathan. She could put her own seatbelt around both of them, better than nothing, she thought, and she would pray she didn't get pulled over.

Almost to the second that she put the car in park at the Carriage House parking lot, her cell phone rang. She looked at the screen, it read Mike Williams. She pressed the 'answer' button and yelled, "Mike!"

She could see him grinning as he replied, "Well hello to you too, what's up?" Elizabeth pulled the phone away from her ear and looked at it with a puzzled look.

"What's up?" she said, "What's up? Really? Mike, where is your son?" She glanced down at Johnathan as silly as it was, to make sure he was still with her.

"He's at day care," Mike replied and as he finished speaking she heard noise in the background. Voices. Music.

"Wrong Mike, they close at six. And where are you?"

"I'm at the Officer's Club, a few of the guys wanted to take me out for a beer to catch up. So really, they close at six?" At that comment her mother pulled in beside her. Elizabeth held one finger up to her, a request to stay put and hold on for a minute. Her mother nodded.

Elizabeth was getting angrier with Mike's every word. "Mike, they close at six, they've been trying to call you and couldn't get an answer. So they called me. I was getting ready for my night class but they told me I had to get over there and pick him up immediately. They said they charge you a dollar a minute for every minute you're late. Did they not tell you all of this when you signed him up?" she nearly screamed at him.

On his end, Mike closed his eyes and rubbed his head, thinking. That's who the unknown number must've been, the daycare, and he'd ignored the calls. "Yeah, yeah, maybe they did, look, I'm sorry. I'll finish my beer and head home, ok?"

Now she was pissed. "You'll finish your beer? Mike, you'll leave now, to hell with your beer, and you'll meet me in the Carriage House parking lot. Why, you ask? Because I don't have a car seat, and I already drove here from the daycare holding your son. Illegally. Now get your ass here pronto," and she hung up on him. For as much compassion and sympathy she had felt for this man until now, she was feeling just as much anger toward him at the moment. She rolled her window down to fill her mother in, yelling louder than she meant to and the baby started crying.

Frustrated, she told her mother thanks for coming but that she should go back home. Her mother nodded but first opened her car door. Elizabeth bounced the baby a little and he stopped crying. "Here honey, take this car seat in case this ever happens again," and she took it from her back seat. She walked around to the front of Elizabeth's car and opened the passenger door. Looking in she said, "Not much room in here for a car seat, is there?" No there wasn't, Elizabeth thought as she shook her head.

"Just put it in the trunk mom," she said as she popped it open from inside the car. Her mother did as

196

she requested, got into her car and waved goodbye with a sympathetic look on her face. Elizabeth assumed the sympathy was for her, but her mother was actually feeling sorry for the lashing Mike would get when he arrived.

Mike showed up a little past 7:30 and until Elizabeth got through with him it was almost 8 PM. He'd just wanted to go relax a little, he'd lost track of time and the men he had been out with were lieutenant colonels and could help him significantly with their advice in regard to his career.

Elizabeth took a good look at Mike's face. Was she seeing the face of a man who would ever understand his responsibilities as not only a father but as a single parent? She couldn't be sure, what she did know was that he hadn't shown it tonight. He apologized a thousand times over but Elizabeth didn't think it was heartfelt, she didn't think he truly understood the severity of leaving your child at day care while you're at a bar regardless if you're with lieutenant colonels or not.

Elizabeth glanced at her watch. Too late to get to class now, it would be 8:15 till she got there and class ended at nine. How ironic. The baby's father is out there trying to enhance his own career while simultaneously screwing hers up. As she watched him retrieve the baby from her arms she felt a twang of sympathy for him. Had she been thinking more clearly she may have felt sorry for Johnathan instead, but Mike did unknowingly pull on her heart strings As much as she missed Amy, she couldn't begin to imagine how he was feeling. He thought he had found his lifetime and now he was single.

She reached out to hug him. "Just don't do it again, ok Mike? I missed my class tonight. You know I love you and the little guy but I have my own life. I don't mind helping out when I know about it ahead of time but this last minute stuff isn't going to fly. Got it?"

Mike looked at her sheepishly. "Yeah, I'm sorry Elizabeth. I'm doing the best I can…" and Elizabeth cut him off.

"Just don't do it again," and with that she got into her car and turned the key in the ignition. She wanted to go home but there was work she could do at school so she headed in that direction. The whole way there she kept thinking about Johnathan, she felt sorry for the poor little guy. She knew Mike loved him but wasn't sure he was ready for this responsibility. What else could he do, though? Amy's parents didn't want the baby, this much was obvious and he couldn't put it up for adoption, could he? Could you do that just because you don't have time for your baby? Surely you couldn't, but she wasn't sure. She tried to push the thoughts from her mind, tried focusing on work and what needed done, but visions of lesson plans on her desk for review continually turned into seeing Johnathan laying in his crib, with a messy diaper, no bottle, the mobile hanging above him, still, and Mike nowhere in sight.

Mike took the baby home, changed him, gave him a bottle and put him to bed. He knew it'd be a short four to six hours until he was up again for more.

198

He turned the television on in the living room and lay down on the couch, making sure the baby monitor was on in case he fell asleep. He'd been having no trouble sleeping but also had no difficulty hearing the baby through the monitor each time he awoke with cries of hunger, wetness, or God knows what.

The next morning he took the baby to daycare and offered his profuse apologies to the Director. She was calmer than the previous night but he wouldn't have known that and she told him it was ok but not to let it happen again. She told him the added charges for late pick-up would appear on his weekly bill and he nodded his understanding. From there he went to work.
Walking in he saw an envelope on his desk, it hadn't been there the night before and he looked at it curiously. Looking around the office he saw a few other soldiers already at their desks working, there were a few empty seats. He walked over to his desk and picked up the envelope. Looking at it first, he wondered where it'd come from. Surely none of his guys would've placed it there. He slid his finger under the flap and opened it, taking out a formal letter from his Commander. As he read he felt eyes upon him and glanced up at his office mates. They were smiling. "Congratulations," the second lieutenant who sat across from him said. Apparently they knew what the letter said based on who'd brought it in. "Looks like your upward bound, sir," and he chuckled a little.
The letter confirmed that he'd been accepted to school in Kansas and it informed him that he had a report date of 5 January. Two and a half months from

today. He inhaled deeply, and then exhaled, and a smile crossed his face. This is what he'd wanted and he was happy, but at the same time he was overwhelmed with all the arrangements he'd have to make between now and then. Making a permanent change of station with the Army was never easy and he couldn't imagine how he'd do it with a baby in his arms. He rubbed his hand through his hair as one of his colleagues clapped him on the back and offered his congratulations. Yeah thanks man, pretty cool," he said. And it hit him that he had no one to tell that would care. No one to celebrate with. No one for him to tell how big this was for him. And the smile faded from his face. He'd text Elizabeth later although he wasn't sure if she was over being pissed at him. Maybe he'd apologize first, again, and then share his news. He wanted someone to be happy for him, someone who didn't wear camouflage.

Chapter Fourteen

*"Lifetime relationships teach you lifetime lessons;
things you must build upon in order to have a solid
emotional foundation. Your   job is to accept the
lesson, love the person, and put what you have learned
to use in all other relationships and areas of your life.
It is said that love is blind but friendship is
clairvoyant." ~Author Unknown*

Elizabeth wasn't sure how much longer this could go
on. It was nearing Thanksgiving and she was busy at
work, as usual. In fact busier than usual since the new
standardized testing had come out and Mike was
calling on her at least five times a week to help with
Johnathan. Sometimes it was a late pick-up at daycare
although he hadn't forgotten his son like the first
incident, sometimes it was to watch the baby at the
apartment while he was sleeping so that Mike could
run errands, sometimes it was so Mike could get out
and have some time to himself, and sometimes it was
to ask for advice which was really ridiculous given
Elizabeth's lack of history with kids. He knew she
could call her mother though and he was surprised at
how on target her answers always were.

However, Elizabeth was growing weary. She couldn't seem to say no to him and what confused her was that she didn't think she wanted to. She'd always cared for Mike and she'd quickly grown to love the little boy and she actually enjoyed spending time with him. She still panicked from time to time but between her mother and searching for information on the Internet she was always able to find out what she needed to know. Each time she looked at him she thought of Amy, not only did he have her eyes and a few other facial features but it just seemed natural. Johnathan represented Amy and at first it made her sad but the more time she spent with him, the more she was glad for the connection. Mike had started packing for his move to Kansas. He was selling their furniture off, even that which had belonged to Amy. It kind of irritated Elizabeth but there was nothing she could do about it. He had planned to get a furnished place in Kansas since they'd only be there for a year and he said he'd worry about buying new furniture when they got to Germany. He was praying that once they got to Germany Amy's parents would take a role in their grandson's life.

The Saturday before Thanksgiving Mike had called on Elizabeth once again. He told her he needed to take care of some paperwork at the office he hadn't gotten done by the deadline and made sure she knew it was because he always had to leave by 5:45 to pick Johnathan up at daycare. She sighed and looked at the mounds of work in front of her, some school work and some college work, and said what she always said.

"On my way." Mike hung up and got the bottles ready. He needed to show Elizabeth how to do this so he wouldn't have to take his time to do so, note to self, he thought.

When she got there he nearly had one foot out the door before she even parked her car. He thanked her quickly and told her the bottles were ready in the fridge. Hold on, she thought, bottles? Plural? Just how long did he plan to be gone? She hollered the question to him before he shut his truck door, his reply came back "couple of hours," and he started the ignition. Elizabeth had wanted to clarify that couple meant two but she was too late, he was gone.

She went straight to Johnathan's room, thank God he hadn't sold any of this furniture and the room was intact. As she always did, she stared at the mural and her eyes frequently moved to the inscription that meant so much to her. She remembered asking Mike how Amy had gotten the landlord to allow her to do it and he said that as long as they painted it back to the original color before he left, it would be fine. It made her sick to think that the mural and Amy's signature would be painted over one day soon.

Johnathan was still asleep but that didn't keep her from standing there staring at him. He was so precious, she didn't know how Mike could not want to spend more time with him. She tried to imagine what he'd look like as he got older, as a toddler, as a little league player, as a teen, and as a man. It made her sad to face the reality that once Mike and the baby left, she'd probably never see Johnathan again. Sure they'd communicate for a little while but she knew how that

203

went, it wouldn't be long until they lost touch. It was entirely possible that Mike would find another woman to marry, giving Johnathan another mom. The thought made Elizabeth cringe.

Glancing at her watch she saw that it was noon. Two hours shouldn't be too bad, she thought, she hadn't brought any work along but she had downloaded a new book on her Kindle recently, something school related about the first days of school. It was a resource to help new teachers and covered more than the first few days but that was the title. She wanted to read all that she could to be able to provide support to new teachers, she remembered all too well what the first year was like. Curling up on the recliner she settled in with her electronic reader, the monitor by her side. She couldn't wait for Johnathan to wake up but until then, she'd gain some wisdom from Mr. Wong.

At 4:00 Elizabeth was a mix of ready to kill Mike and ready to pull her hair out. He hadn't come back, apparently couple didn't mean two and he didn't answer any of the 20 or so calls or texts she'd attempted. Johnathan, despite having been fed, burped, and changed, was having a crying fit. Some might call it screaming. She'd read a little bit about colic and wondered if this was it. As she attempted to rock him on the recliner, her Kindle caught her eye. Hey Mr. Wong, she thought, how about writing a book called the first days of childcare? She certainly could use it right about now. She tried walking the floor with him, bouncing him in her arms. She even tried laying him back down thinking he was tired. Nothing worked. Looking at the window in hopes of seeing Mike's truck pull in, she spotted only her own car.

Then it dawned on her that she still had the car seat her mother had brought her in her trunk. She bundled the crying Johnathan up, grabbed her coat, and took off out the door. She checked to make sure the door didn't lock behind her since she didn't have a key, then proceeded to get the car seat out of her trunk and somehow managed to get Johnathan strapped into it in the backseat. She didn't know if she'd done it right or not but he was in. Telling herself 'that wasn't so hard,' she couldn't help feeling a little sense of pride as she jumped into the passenger seat and started the Camaro. Her mother's house was only about two miles away, she'd know how to quiet the baby, and Elizabeth headed that way. She turned the music on to drown out the wailing, she didn't want to turn it too loud and hurt the baby's ears but she needed some relief and loud music was better than loud screaming.

As she turned the corner to her mother's street she turned the music down and prepared to pull into the driveway. Slowing to a stop it dawned on her. No screaming. No noise whatsoever, complete quiet except for the sound of the car engine. Panicking a little she turned and looked to make sure he was ok and saw his little head turned into the car seat, the blanket over his little chest which was slowly heaving up and down. Yes, he was alive and breathing, he was ok, he was just sleeping! Had he tired himself out from all the crying or had he just gotten sleepy? She didn't know and she didn't care as she backed out of the driveway and went for a very long drive.

A few minutes past six her cell rang. Looking first toward the baby to see if it had awakened him, she then grabbed her cell. Mike Williams. She contemplated not answering, let him see how it feels, but she couldn't do that. After all she did have his child in her car. As she answered the phone she turned her car around to head back towards Mike's apartment, she'd drop Johnathan off and head back home to take care of some of her work. "Hey Mike, don't panic, your son's fine, we just went for a little ride, we're on the way home," she said and waited for his response. Her anger of his lateness and the crying had dissipated, the drive had done her good. She waited for his sigh of relief, she assumed he'd gotten home and panicked when they weren't there. Mike spoke quickly.

"Oh hey, you're out and about? That's great, well listen, don't hurry, my work took a little longer than I thought it would and when I was leaving I ran into some of the guys, we're going to go grab a bite to eat. I shouldn't be too long, that ok with you?"

Elizabeth was at a loss for words. She couldn't believe what she was hearing. She opened her mouth to speak but had no idea what words would come out. Those that did let him know in no uncertain terms that she was headed to his house now and if he knew what was good for him he'd be there waiting. She had to check her speed to make sure her anger hadn't been transferred to her right foot but she was well within the limits. It seemed she had subconsciously put little

Johnathan's safety and well-being first which was more than she could say she'd do for that father of his.

The interaction between Mike and Elizabeth was quick and quiet. It appeared Mike had known what was in his best interest and Elizabeth found him standing on the front steps when she pulled up to his apartment. She carefully unstrapped the buckles and pulled the still-sleeping Johnathan from the car seat. The look on her face told Mike not to speak, and he didn't, he simply held his arms out to take the baby from Elizabeth and then watched her storm back toward her car. The anger had returned, not for the same reason it had existed earlier but for the nerve of Mike. He had no respect for her or her time. She was just about to her car when she stopped. Mike watched as she stood silently for a few seconds, then she turned on her heel and marched right back up the sidewalk.

"Mike Williams do you love your son?" Mike nodded. "Do you? Are you sure? Do you really? I mean Mike, you are about to take this child with you to another state thousands of miles away where you will have no support. I won't be there Mike, do you get that? I won't be there! What will you do when you have to work late? Who will you call when you need to run errands and can't or don't want to take the baby with you? Hmm? Who's going to help you with all the questions you have? And what about when you just want to go out and have a few beers with the boys, Mike? And in case you've forgotten you're going to be in school. Mike, you're going to have long days with homework at night. How are you going to take care of Johnathan with all of that going on? Have you thought about all of that Mike? Because you sure as hell don't act like you have."

Somewhere in the middle of her tirade tears began to well in Mike's eyes. He stood and heard her out and then turned to enter the apartment. He's not getting off this easy, Elizabeth thought and she followed him inside. She started in on him again as soon as he'd returned from putting Johnathan in his crib. By her calculations he should sleep about another 30 minutes and then be ready for a bottle but then what did she know? She was just the nanny, at least that's what she felt like.

She'd been about five words into her next speech when Mike held a hand up to her. He looked at her and his eyes begged her to stop. She stopped and they stared at each other intently. Slowly they lowered themselves to sit on the couch, side by side. Mike reached out and took Elizabeth's hand. He knew what he wanted to say but wasn't sure how to say it, he wasn't sure if Elizabeth would slap him in the face or hug him with happiness. He took several deep breaths before he spoke, Elizabeth started wondering what was going to come out of his mouth. If she didn't know better she'd think he was going to hit on her but this was Mike, Amy's boyfriend. Amy. Amy, her best friend. Surely he wouldn't do something so dumb, would he? But then Mike hadn't been making the most rational decisions lately, had he? Feeling uncomfortable, she pulled her hand from his and leaned back on the couch so they weren't so close. Mike spoke first.

"Elizabeth I have an idea. I know it may sound crazy but please hear me out. I'm trying to figure out a way to manage everything and stay sane and this is the only thing I could come up with. Please, hear me out."

Elizabeth listened, and then nodded. "Go ahead," she told him.

"Elizabeth I loved Amy, I probably always will, I don't think there will ever be another woman for me." He sniffed a little before continuing. "That being said, you know my plans for the Army, I want to advance as far as I can and that takes a lot of time and commitment on my behalf." Elizabeth nodded knowing all too well about time and commitment but wasn't quite sure where he was headed with the conversation. "Elizabeth I know your career is important to you too, more than anything else, I know and respect that. But you have to have a life too, where does that come in? All you ever do is work, work, work."

It was Elizabeth's turn to talk. "That's the way I want it Mike, I'm making the choice to live that way and if I don't mind not having a social life, why should you care?" She made a valid point but Mike had come this far with the sharing of his plan and he couldn't stop now.

"I know Elizabeth but I think that if you took some time to yourself, to do some of the things you like to do, to spend some time with Johnathan, you might find you enjoy it. I don't think you know what you're missing," he said.

She startled back with a surprised look on her face. "How much more time do you want me to spend with him, Mike? Between daycare and me, it's you that doesn't spend much time with him." Mike's face fell a little with that comment, he knew it was true but he continued.

"Elizabeth, I have an idea, some might call it a business proposition or a contract agreement, hell I don't know, but what if you and I get married?" She wondered if the look on her face showed the actual amount of shock she was feeling that second or just a portion of it. She couldn't even speak. "I mean hear me out, we get married on paper only, which brings you under my military benefits, which are pretty damn good. You and I and Johnathan move to Kansas and then Germany. You can get a job teaching over there, it wouldn't make sense to get one for a year in Kansas but once we'd get to Germany I know some people who work for DODS, and you can continue your schooling online. I can do my schooling in Kansas and work toward my promotion in Germany. I'll probably have to deploy again at some point but we'd be married and you'd have everything you'd need, the military provides for its own."

Elizabeth felt her head swarming. He'd really thought this through, my God he even has me enrolling in online courses, she thought. She looked around the room as if searching for a camera and someone yelling 'ha-ha, we got you' yet she continued staring at Mike.

"Elizabeth I know you love Johnathan and I wouldn't ever expect you to love me, we'd even have separate bedrooms, but I think this is best for him. I would need an answer soon Elizabeth, because we'd have to get a marriage license and get everything set up before we leave here, it's easier that way, but we have a month before we'd have to go, we have enough time. I've been thinking about this for weeks and I swear it's the only way I can think of to be a father to him and not lose my own dreams."

Elizabeth stood up, taking her eyes off Mike for the first time since he began talking. She looked around the apartment, what was left of Amy's furniture and things, and then she walked toward the baby's room. When she reached the doorway she stopped dead in her tracks. She shook her head slightly but it was unmistakable, she was having a flashback. Like it was yesterday, she remembered the party they'd attended when she was married to Lance, the one where she'd found him in the nursery, the tiny baby girl bundled in his arms. She remembered hearing him cooing to the baby and the baby looking at him as if she understood him. As impossible as it was, she swore she could hear the soft music of the mobile that hung above the baby girl's crib. The memory made her smile. Maybe Lance hadn't been so crazy after all, maybe a baby could bring you happiness. She lifted her feet one by one and slowly, gently, moved herself toward Johnathan's crib. He'd awakened at some point but had not made a sound, if he had they'd have heard it from the monitor in the living room. He looked up at Elizabeth and she could've sworn the corners of his mouth curled into a smile. Glancing up at the jungle mobile above his crib, she clicked the button on and listened as the soft music played. Gazing into Johnathan's eyes she realized it was the same lullaby she'd heard from the mobile in the baby girl's crib just

211

a few years ago. She wiped the tears that had started to fall down her face as she turned to face the mural Amy had painted.

She walked towards the mural while the music played in the background, she thought she'd heard Johnathan cooing a little too but she wasn't sure. Facing the mural, she ran her hand over the jungle animals once gain and allowed her fingers to slide their way toward the inscription that she loved, 'Johnathan Michael, You are my lifetime. Love, Mommy'. Kneeling down, she moved her fingertips from the mural to her lips. Thinking only of her best friend, she slowly kissed her fingertips and then, just as slowly, moved her hand back to place the kiss onto the inscription. She nodded her head and smiled. A contract. Separate bedrooms. Lifetime benefits. It all swarmed in her head. Without a hesitation in the world, she wiped her tear-stained face and stood up. Blowing a final kiss to Johnathan, she walked confidently out of the baby's room. She knew what she had to do.

TWO MONTHS LATER

Elizabeth instinctively smiled as she opened her eyes to the sunlight streaming through her bedroom window. Glancing at the clock she saw that it was 6:14 AM. Days of working at the Carriage House flashed before her eyes and she laughed to herself. Those were the days, she thought. But that was then, this was now, and these days she had a different reason to smile. In the past two months her world had taken a complete turn, one that was not expected but one that had changed her life for the better. She yawned a yawn that always seemed to be left from the night before, she stretched her arms over her head with a slight groan, and shook her body awake. She had to stop to think about what day it was, Saturday, and she smiled when she realized it.

Leaping out of bed, not wanting to waste another moment of the day, she walked down the hall and into his room, quiet so as not to wake him this early. She had learned that he liked to sleep in, she never would've guessed it about him but she did like to indulge him that little pleasure. Tiptoeing into his room she looked around, it was sparsely decorated but he didn't seem to mind. Little did he know she had plans to change that as early as this afternoon, and she knew he'd love it. She moved toward him as he slept, wondering how late it would be this morning and smiled when she got close enough to see the details of his face. How could she have grown to care for him so much in such a short period of time? Feeling selfish, she decided she couldn't wait any longer, she wanted him to wake up and begin enjoying the day with her. What would they do today, she wondered? Every day was an adventure with him, always something new; Mike had been right, she hadn't known what she was missing by making work her priority. She leaned down and kissed his face, hoping to wake him, and it worked. At first he stirred just a little, unsure he was ready to face the day just yet but when she kissed him again his eyes opened wide and he smiled that smile she'd grown to love. "Good morning my sweet baby," she said to Johnathan as he cooed and smiled and reached his arms toward her.

After changing his diaper, she carried her son out to the kitchen and sat him in his highchair as she prepared his bottle. Some mornings he got a little bit of cereal at breakfast but not today, she wanted to hold him and rock him and love him. It was going to be a special day for them and she couldn't wait. While the bottle was warming she looked around the living room of her townhouse. Gone were the expensive trinkets and statues, in their place were a baby swing, a playpen, and more toys than a toy store could hold. Elizabeth smiled, what a difference two months had made, she thought. The microwave dinged and she took the bottle out. Before retrieving the baby from the highchair and moving to the rocker she'd brought from Amy and Mike's apartment, she grabbed the mail. Mail was something she'd let accumulate for days and then go through all at once.

With Johnathan, the bottle, and the mail in hand, she settled in for her favorite part of the day, feeding him. Johnathan spotted the bottle and began the noise making that ensued every time he saw his bottle. She loved the sounds he made, each one, and she made a mental note to record some of them on her phone. Cradling him and placing the bottle in his mouth, Elizabeth reached for her first piece of mail. It was a thick envelope. Turning it over to the front she saw that it was from the lawyer's office. These would be the final papers that she and Mike had drawn up and agreed upon a few days after his well-intended proposal of marriage. Without realizing it she leaned down and kissed her son on his forehead as he drank his bottle. She opened the envelope and read over the material, yes, it all seemed to be what they'd discussed, and as soon as she was done feeding him she'd sign it and send her copies back. She was quite sure that in Kansas, Mike would be doing the same thing.

She recalled their conversation in his apartment that day after she walked out of the baby's room. He was still sitting on the couch, head hung down, not sure what to expect from Elizabeth as she walked toward him. Part of him wanted to duck, part of him wanted to run, but he stayed put and waited for her response. She'd told him that she thought he was very noble for trying to do the right thing for his son, albeit a bit unorthodox. He had assured her it happened in the military more often than she could imagine but she responded that she didn't care and that she had a counter offer for him.

She made it very clear to him that she would not be marrying him or moving to Kansas and then Germany. She then had a long conversation with him about the responsibilities of parenthood and each time she asked him, "can you do that with no help?" and then, "do you want to do that with no help?" Each time his answer was no. Through their conversation Mike was able to admit that not only could he not take care of his son given his career goals, he also wasn't so sure he wanted to. He loved his son and wanted to be a part of his life but Johnathan reminded him too much of Amy and he couldn't stand it.

As he cried he admitted that he sometimes wished Amy had survived instead of the baby. The autopsy had come back and it had been a pulmonary embolism that took her life and while that wasn't good news, they had all been glad to hear it hadn't been a result of the pregnancy for this exact reason, no one wanted Mike to unrealistically blame the baby. Mike told Elizabeth how much he admired her for being able to look past the fact that Johnathan was a reminder of Amy. She said she didn't look past it, she looked at it as a blessing. It was like having a part of Amy still with her.

They talked awhile longer and then Mike asked what her counter offer was, he was desperate for an answer. Elizabeth had been smart enough to realize that it was his desperation that had caused him to make his offer of marriage to her in the first place, he was grasping at the only straws he could see. Elizabeth settled back on the couch to share her idea while Mike listened intently. She proposed that she take full and

216

legal guardianship of Johnathan. She said she would never want or expect him to give up his paternal rights, he needed to be there for his son and he could do that without living with him every day, divorced parents did it successfully all the time. By no means did she feel it was ideal but she was also thinking of what was best for Johnathan and while she didn't know if that was her, she knew it wasn't living with an absentee father. She added that by staying with her, Johnathan would have immediate grandparents who would welcome him with open arms as well as aunts and uncles and lots of cousins to play with.

Mike was listening intently. She went on to say they'd have to have legal paperwork created and said she'd consult with Mike on all major decisions regarding Johnathan. She said there were a million other details they'd have to work out, like Mike providing some financial support but they could do that with the lawyers. Mike seemed to like the idea but had one question – what about her own availability due to her busy and growing career? He could tell this was a tough question for her and he waited patiently for her response which he could tell she was wording in her head, cautiously. She finally spoke and shared that she'd be willing to put her career on hold to raise Johnathan. She would go back to teaching, take an online course here or there, and eventually she'd graduate with her administrative degree. Laughing, she said the hardest part would be trading in her Camaro, it was not conducive to holding a car seat. She told him she didn't know when, where, or how the world turned for her but it had and she'd realized what was important.

Her final words to him regarding her proposal were that she'd be honored to raise her best friend's son and that brought tears to both of them. Mike had asked her if she thought him agreeing made him a bad father. She wasn't sure what to say but the words that came out of her mouth assured him that she felt he'd be making the best decision for his son. In the end he agreed. They'd gone to a lawyer, together, one who would act in both of their best interests but more importantly, in Johnathan's, and the results were in her hand now.

The doorbell rang promptly at 10 AM and while she was expecting him, the noise startled her. She'd been doing some dishes while Johnathan played in his playpen. Reaching to wipe her hands on a dish towel nearby, she smiled and went to let him in. This was a big day for her and Johnathan, one that she had looked forward to since she saw his ad in the newspaper. She'd met with him shortly afterward and now here he was entering her living room. They exchanged pleasantries and she moved to the playpen to pick Johnathan up. "Sweetie," she said to him, "mommy has a big surprise for you. Let's go see what it is!"

She asked the man if he needed anything before he got started and he said no, he had everything with him and was ready to begin, it was going to be a full day's job. She walked back the hallway carrying the baby, grabbing her cell phone on the way. The man followed her with his things, looking around the townhouse and thinking of all he could do here. For now though, he'd focus on the project at hand.

As they entered the baby's room, Elizabeth pulled up the photos on her phone. There were 17 photos altogether that she'd been able to snap before it was too late. She'd captured every detail, leaving nothing to the imagination. The man looked through the pictures as Elizabeth scrolled, nodding his head each time the frame changed. He'd already seen them once and had taken copious notes, he felt very confident in his ability to complete the task to Elizabeth's satisfaction. He sat his materials down and looked around the room. "Yes, this is going to work well, I think you'll be delighted," he said, then leaning toward Johnathan who was propped in Elizabeth's arms he asked, "And who is this handsome fella?"

Elizabeth held the baby tightly but moved him a little closer to the man. "This is my son Johnathan," she said, "Johnathan say hello to Mr. Cotter, he's an artist, and he's going to put a mural in your room just like the one your mommy painted for you before you were born."

As hard as it was, Elizabeth stayed out of the baby's room all day. She'd put Johnathan down for his naps in his playpen to avoid going into the room. She'd brought a supply of diapers and wipes out earlier in the day so she wouldn't have that excuse either. She didn't want to see the mural until it was completely done and at 8:30 PM, Mr. Cotter came out into the living room and said he was done. She got her checkbook out and paid him.

"Don't you want to see it first?" he asked, very surprised to be paid for work that hadn't been previewed.

She shook her head. "No, I'm sure it's fine, my son and I will go see it as soon as you leave, just the two of us." Mr. Cotter smiled and nodded, telling her to call him if she had any concerns but added that if he did say so himself, it was one of the best pieces he'd ever done. She closed the door behind him as he left and exhaled slowly. She looked at Johnathan and said, "Let's go, little man."

She picked him up from amongst his toys and headed toward his room. This was a very emotional moment for her. Amy had worked so hard on the original mural and Elizabeth wanted Johnathan to have something that he could remember his birth mother by for as long as he wanted it on his wall.

They walked into the bedroom, the smell of paint lingering in the air. It had been too cold to open the windows so he'd have to sleep in Elizabeth's room for a day or two as the fans ran in his. She didn't mind, though. As she reached to turn the light switch on, she hesitated. What if it wasn't good, not what she remembered, what if the signature didn't match? She let her doubt get the better of her for about ten more seconds and then, with a 'tah-dah' directed toward her son, she flipped the light switch on.

There before them was the jungle mural and Elizabeth knew immediately that if you didn't know any better, you'd think you were standing in the baby's room from Amy and Mike's old apartment looking at the original. It was absolutely perfect. The trees, she

220

could've sworn the leaves were hanging at the exact lengths and angles of the original. The gray elephant was standing there, still smiling the same way he had in the original. She saw the tiger with the black stripes standing next to the lion who still looked as harmless as he had in the original. She talked about each animal, stopping to make the noises each animal makes, and she heard Johnathan laughing at her noises.

"And now," she said to Johnathan, "the most important part of the mural," as her fingers wandered down to the signature, which was perfect in every way. "Your mama's words to you," and she read them aloud to him. "Johnathan Michael, You are my lifetime. Love, Mommy."

As she said the words she felt like she should be crying, but she wasn't. She looked at the words again as Johnathan made noise of his own and she told herself he was talking to Amy. She ran her fingers over the words and read each one aloud, again. When she got to the end of the inscription her fingers stopped on the last two words - a lifetime. She looked at her son and then back at the words – a lifetime. She hadn't thought about it for a while but as she looked into her son's eyes, Amy's son's eyes, she realized that Amy was there. Amy would always be there, forever. And then it hit her. It had taken until now but it finally hit her. She'd been right all along, she just didn't know it. This was what it felt like, sheer and utter peace and happiness. Elizabeth hugged the boy closely and kissed his face. Through this boy, the one Elizabeth would raise as her son, and from the grave, Amy had proven to be Elizabeth's lifetime

COMING SOON

Second Chances
(the sequel to a Reason, A Season, A Lifetime)

About the Author

Dr. Traci Smith was born and raised in Pennsylvania.
She has earned a Doctorate Degree in Innovations &
Leadership, a Master's Degree in Educational
Administration and a Bachelor of Science in
Education. She has over 30 years of experience serving

public education as a principal, grant writer and teacher. She is also a teacher/mentor to online doctoral students. She currently resides in San Antonio, Texas with her three chocolate labs.

Follow Traci on Facebook:
https://www.facebook.com/tes101162
E-mail: tesmith62@aol.com

Made in United States
Troutdale, OR
09/07/2023

12728345R00141